"We'd make lovely children together."

The astounded look in Nick's eyes had Bernadette quickly adding, "Hypothetically speaking, that is."

He took a deep breath and released it slowly. "Hypothetically speaking," he repeated, "they would be lovely."

Her brown eyes were full of warmth and something else Nick couldn't quite describe. Could it be caring? Was it possible?

Bernadette rested her cheek against his and gave herself up to the music and the pleasure of his touch.

If Nick had any sense at all he'd step away from her, end the dance and be on his way home. But home was that cold monstrosity of a house with no one in it. He didn't want to leave Bernadette and face its emptiness. He didn't want to leave Bernadette... plain and simple.

Dear Reader,

Welcome to Silhouette—experience the magic of the wonderful world where two people fall in love. Meet heroines that will make you cheer for their happiness, and heroes (be they the boy next door or a handsome, mysterious stranger) who will win your heart. Silhouette Romance reflects the magic of love—sweeping you away with books that will make you laugh and cry, heartwarming, poignant stories that will move you time and time again.

In the coming months we're publishing romances by many of your all-time favorites, such as Diana Palmer, Brittany Young, Sondra Stanford and Annette Broadrick. Your response to these authors and our other Silhouette Romance authors has served as a touchstone for us, and we're pleased to bring you more books with Silhouette's distinctive medley of charm, wit and—above all—*romance*.

I hope you enjoy this book and the many stories to come. Experience the magic!

Sincerely,

Tara Hughes
Senior Editor
Silhouette Books

STELLA BAGWELL

Teach Me

Silhouette Romance

Published by Silhouette Books New York

America's Publisher of Contemporary Romance

To Bob and Janice,
for payment due...

SILHOUETTE BOOKS
300 E. 42nd St., New York, N.Y. 10017

ISBN: 0-373-08657-1

First Silhouette Books printing June 1989

Printed in the U.S.A.

STELLA BAGWELL

is a small-town girl and an incurable romantic—a combination she feels enhances her writing. When she isn't at her typewriter she enjoys reading, listening to music, sketching pencil drawings and sewing her own clothes. Most of all she enjoys exploring the outdoors with her husband and young son.

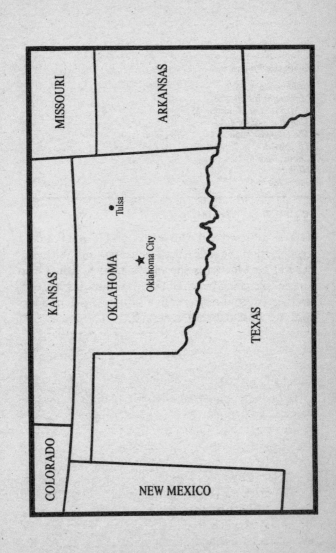

Chapter One

Bernadette Baxter was late and out of breath, all because her alarm clock had chosen this morning, of all mornings, to go on the blink.

Several male heads turned her way as she dodged around and between people and tables wedged in the small pastry shop. It was a regular morning haunt of the businessmen and women who worked in the nearby blocks of office buildings.

Bernadette supposed that for many of the customers, getting a good dose of caffeine and sugar at the start of the day was the reason for coming here. It was downright hunger that brought her to Maria's Donuts every morning of the work week. That, and an incurable craving for sweets.

"Where have you been? Do you know you've got less than fifteen minutes to eat and get to the office?" Joyce asked when Bernadette finally reached the table where her friend sat.

"I know, Joyce, you don't have to remind me," she said with breathless irritation. She pulled out a cushioned wooden chair, sank down on it and inhaled deeply. "My alarm didn't go off!"

"I thought you usually woke up on your own," Joyce said, eyeing her across the table.

"I do," Bernadette replied with a sigh. "But I was exhausted last night. Page and I went dancing and I didn't get home till two."

Just as Bernadette was pulling off her coat, a waitress appeared at her elbow. "Give me two raisin-cinnamon rolls and a coffee," Bernadette told her.

Nodding, the waitress hurried away.

Joyce said, "Are you—no, you're not talking about Page Sayer, who plays running back for OU?" Her face was a picture of astonishment as Bernadette nodded. "Berny, how did you two ever get together?"

Bernadette shrugged with nonchalance and thanked the waitress, who had returned to place her order on the tiny table. "Let's see, it was at one of Nigel's parties, I think. Page was a friend of someone who was there. We just happened to bump into each other."

Frowning with pure disgust, Joyce leaned back in her chair. "And that's all it took? Just a bump, and you wind up dancing all night with him. I could have paraded by the guy stark naked and he wouldn't have noticed me!"

Bernadette swallowed a bite of cinnamon roll, then laughed. "Joyce! There's no big deal about Page. He's merely a guy."

"Merely a guy who is known nationwide, who is probably in the running for the Heisman Trophy. A guy who is nothing but slabs of muscles and—" Her eyes narrowed curiously on Bernadette. "By the way, he's kinda young for you, isn't he?"

"Hmm, well, not really. He's not that much younger. Two or three years. I think he's twenty-two. What does it matter?"

Joyce was twenty-eight, divorced and worked at the same insurance company as Bernadette. For two years, they'd worked together in the same typing pool, then Joyce had been transferred to data processing while Bernadette had somehow managed to move up the ladder to become private secretary of the executive vice president of sales. It wasn't fair! But then Joyce was not the only woman to look at Bernadette and find herself repeating those words.

It wasn't fair for anyone to have hair as naturally blond as that. And it certainly wasn't fair for anyone to go through so many sweets and still have a figure that turned heads and raised temperatures. It didn't stop there, either. Bernadette had beautiful blue eyes that glowed and complemented her flaxen hair. Her complexion was flawless, her lips just full enough to give them that pouty, kissable look. Not to mention the perfect lines of her nose and cheeks. It was no wonder the woman never lacked for male attention.

Yet there was something else about Berny besides her looks that drew men to her. Joyce couldn't quite put her finger on what it was, but once she discovered it, she planned to bottle it and make her first million.

"What does it matter? Well, I guess it wouldn't to you," Joyce said dryly. "After all, love 'em and leave 'em is your motto, isn't it? Or at least change them around every few days so they won't get too hung up on you."

Bernadette flung out her hand in a dismissive gesture and knocked over her coffee cup. "Oh, darn it!" She groaned and looked down at her new striped tie now splattered with the dark liquid. She grabbed a napkin, dunked it in her water glass, then used it to wipe out the stains. "I hope this doesn't mean the rest of my day is going to go like this! We're starting on our quarterly reports today, and Mr. Atwood is always edgy until we get them finished."

"Always edgy," the brunette repeated mockingly. "I'd say that man is a walking straight razor."

Bernadette clucked her tongue. "Joyce, Mr. Atwood is a very nice boss. You know he saw to it personally that I received a raise this year."

"Yeah, well, it was probably because of all those miniskirts you wear. More than likely he heard your legs were insured with Lloyd's and thought you might need the extra money for premiums."

"Joyce," Bernadette scolded lightly. "Mr. Atwood would hardly know if I had one or two legs. A womanizer he is not."

Joyce laughed dryly while rolling her dirty napkin into a tight little ball. "That cold stuffed shirt with a woman? I'll bet he takes his corporate reports to bed with him every night."

"He's very brilliant," Bernadette felt compelled to say.

"In what department?"

"Oh, please," Bernadette groaned and took one last sip of coffee. "We'd better get to work. It's five till. I should have already been there."

Both women paid at the counter, then stepped out onto the sidewalk and into thirty-degree weather. Bernadette pulled up the collar of her white fur coat to ward off the icy wind that plummeted the chill factor to minus degrees. It was whirling and sucking through the concrete valley created by the skyscrapers towering on either side of the street.

Oklahoma City could be miserable in December, and this one was proving to be no exception. Bernadette thought that if it had to be this cold, at least they should have snow for Christmas, which was only about two weeks away.

Joyce enviously eyed the coat wrapped around her friend. "That's the coat your mother got you for your last birthday, isn't it?"

Bernadette nodded, a smile tilting her lips. "Sweet of her, wasn't it?"

"Very sweet," Joyce agreed. "But it would take more than a coat to make the opposite sex look at me the way they look at you."

Frowning, Bernadette said, "I don't ask men to look at me, Joyce."

"You don't have to ask," Joyce went on. "They just naturally look."

Bernadette cast her friend a rueful glance. "What is it with you today? Why all the nasty little innuendos?"

Joyce grinned devilishly. "Probably because I've spent the last three weekends alone, and probably because looking at you every morning makes me feel like an old shoe for the rest of the day."

Bernadette laughed throatily and gave Joyce's arm an affectionate shake. "Cheer up, old friend. Christmas is coming and the new year is on its way! I feel something exciting in the air."

Joyce's nose wrinkled up at the gray sky over their heads. "Yeah, and I think it's sleet."

Bernadette giggled. "Come on. We'd better make a run for it. I'm going to be late!"

Standing in his office doorway, Nicholas Atwood caught the tap-tapping of high heels sprinting across the tiled corridor long before the door to the outer office opened and Miss Baxter hurried in with an apologetic smile on her face.

"Good morning, Mr. Atwood. Sorry I'm late," she said. "I hope you haven't been waiting long." The cream-colored challis skirt swirled around her calves as she turned and hung her coat on a stand in one corner of the room.

He pushed his black-rimmed glasses farther up on his nose and stepped into her part of the office. "It's all right, Miss Baxter. I've been going over the reports. I managed to finish some of them last night."

Bernadette smiled at him as she crossed to her desk and sat down. She pulled her glasses out of their case and slipped them on her face. Poor man, she thought, he was home working on reports while she'd been out dancing and enjoying herself. But then Mr. Atwood received a phenomenal paycheck. Maybe she'd be willing to turn in her dancing shoes for that amount of money. She doubted it. Money couldn't compensate for *everything*. "Then I take it you'll be wanting to work on those after you go through your correspondence?" she asked.

He nodded and thrust his hands in the front pockets of his trousers. For some reason, Bernadette thought about Joyce's comments about her boss. Cold? Stuffed shirt? Funny, she'd never thought of him in exactly that way. She knew everyone who worked at Sooner Fidelity thought of him that way.

Yet ninety-five percent of those people didn't know him. Actually she didn't think anyone really knew him, or at least anyone here at the insurance company. He was sort of a recluse. She'd never once heard him mention family or friends. It was always business with Mr. Atwood, nothing more or less.

For one rare moment, she let herself look at him in a physical way. He was not a bad-looking guy. In fact, if he paid a little attention to fashion and a few other minor details, he could be a real cutie. Not a hunk like Page Sayer by any means, but still...

Well, all men had *something* about them, she silently defended her thoughts as she imagined how much Joyce would laugh if she could only see what Bernadette was thinking. Mr. Atwood a cutie—it was a riot!

She pulled her chair behind the huge metal desk, adjusted her glasses to the proper position on her nose and reached for a letter opener. Mr. Atwood's shadow fell on the desktop and she looked up inquiringly. He usually stayed in his office at this time of the day, tending to the dozen calls he referred to as important. The other two dozen or so were left for Bernadette to either answer or ignore.

"Was there something else?" she asked sweetly.

"Er, yes, there is something I'd like to discuss with you before we get started today."

Bernadette's fine brows arched behind the tortoiseshell frames of her glasses. He sounded so serious. "Oh, I hope I haven't made a mess of something," she voiced anxiously.

In spite of Bernadette's busy social life and errant pursuit of fun, she was a dedicated secretary. She took great pride in her work and strove to be one of the most efficient workers at Sooner Fidelity.

"Not in the least," he said briskly. "You always do a fine job, Miss Atwood. This has... this is something entirely different."

This surprised Bernadette even more, yet she managed to maintain the pleasant professional expression on her face. "Would you like me to fetch you a cup of coffee? It will only take a second."

He nodded. "Thank you, Miss Atwood. I'll be in my office when you return." He crossed the room and shut the door behind him.

For a second, Bernadette stared at it with a faint frown, then quickly pushed her chair away from the desk.

Well, it looked like today was definitely on a different track, she thought. First her alarm, then sopping her new tie, being late, and now Mr. Atwood acting totally out of character. She wondered what could possibly be next.

The coffee room was only a few yards down the hallway from her and Mr. Atwood's office. She quickly made her way down to the little lounge and poured a Styrofoam cup full of coffee.

"Hello, Berny," a male voice sounded behind her. She turned, already knowing it was Nigel, a fast-talking, red-haired flirt who worked in data with Joyce and several others. "You look splendid this morning, as usual."

"Thank you, Nigel. You're looking rather splendid yourself," she said with a saucy grin while reaching with her free hand to pull his striped suspender. She released it, and it hit his chest with a loud pop.

Nigel yelped and rubbed the spot, his eyes fixed on Bernadette's face. "Needing a fix of caffeine after your night with Page?" he asked coyly.

Bernadette pulled a face. "I'm wide awake, thank you. This is for Mr. Atwood. Besides, who told you about Page?"

"Darling Berny, you know this place would be as boring as dead lice if we didn't have your social life to talk about."

Her smile was threatening. "What did I do to deserve a friend like you, Nigel?"

He laughed and took great pleasure in patting her cheek. "You sweet thing. By the way, how is freezer-face this morning?"

Frowning, she stepped around him. "Don't call him that," she said. "Mr. Atwood is the best boss I've ever had."

Nigel chuckled under his breath as he followed Bernadette out of the room. "I can well imagine. He's the only boss who hasn't chased you around the desk. And from wimpy Atwood's record, I doubt you'll ever have that problem."

Bernadette increased her pace, making her heels tap out a fast rhythm on the Italian tile. "Go to work, Nigel. You're making me nauseous," she tossed over her shoulder.

He laughed and blew her a kiss as she stepped into her office and shut the door behind her.

Bernadette knocked and entered Mr. Atwood's private domain. Her boss was sitting behind a massive desk, his chair swiveled toward an expanse of plate glass that formed one wall of the office. He was simply staring out at the tall, modern buildings shrouded by a gray winter haze of clouds.

"Here you are, Mr. Atwood. Black, just like you like it."

She set the cup carefully on the ink pad on his desk. He looked up and turned the chair around so that he was facing her.

"Thank you, Miss Baxter," he said, lifting the cup. "You don't have to do this though, you know. I'm not one of those bosses who think their secretaries are go-fers."

"Of course not," she said, smiling. "And it hardly makes me feel used to fetch you a cup of coffee."

Mr. Atwood motioned toward the chair that Bernadette always used when taking dictation. "Please have a seat, Miss Baxter."

Bernadette sat primly on the heavy wooden chair beside his desk, smoothing her skirt as she looked across at him. He really has nice hair, she thought. It was a dark coffee-color, and it glinted with shiny highlights when the light caught it. All it really needed was a good cut by Richard, her longtime hairdresser. He could do wonders with that thick hair, which was now merely parted and slicked back perfectly to one side.

Her gaze left his hair and traveled downward to his eyes. His eyes were—well, Bernadette had a suspicion they were a vivid shade of blue, but they were blurred by his glasses. Then there was his mouth to consider. The only thing Bernadette could find wrong with it was that it never curved into a smile. Maybe it curved with a faint one at times, but never a true, wide smile, born out of genuine pleasure.

Bernadette blinked as it dawned on her that she had been staring and he had yet to say a word. No wonder he had such a strange look on his face, she thought, shifting in her chair. He was probably wondering if she'd taken leave of her senses inspecting him in such a way! "Will I need my dictation pad for this?" she asked for want of anything else to say.

He shook his head and took a sip of the hot coffee. "No. Actually this is something personal," he said briskly.

Bernadette hoped she didn't look as shocked as she felt. Mr. Atwood had never discussed anything personal with her. In fact, these past two years that she'd worked for him, he'd been so impersonal that she sometimes forgot he existed outside of these office walls. But then maybe it wasn't pertaining to him. Maybe he was going to discuss the fact that a few of her male friends had called her here at the office. Or maybe how he didn't like the idea of flowers being delivered to her on work premises.

"I—is something wrong?" she asked, getting slightly irritated because he wouldn't get on with it. If he planned on giving her a lecture, he might as well begin.

"No, Miss Baxter, it's, well, I don't really know how to approach you about this," he said, making Bernadette's eyes widen with surprise.

Nicholas swallowed and let his gaze travel over her hair. It was always so soft and gently curved under on her shoulders. Uneven bangs brushed her forehead. Little red earrings dangled from her lobes and peeked from beneath her hair whenever she moved her head. He knew as he looked at her that he had made the right choice.

Nicholas prided himself in his judgment of people and business. From long training, he had disciplined himself to weigh all angles and make his decisions with cool, careful logic. This time was no different, even though his goal was a bit out of character for him. Yet it would work, he knew, if everything went as planned and he could get a little help from the Big Man up there.

"Why don't you just jump in with both feet?" Bernadette suggested with a bright smile.

He responded to her words with a faint smile. Actually it was just a faint quirk of one, but Bernadette had known him long enough to decipher his facial expressions. She felt much better after the little smile. Maybe he wasn't going to lecture her after all.

"Yes, perhaps you're right," he replied, then set the Styrofoam cup down.

Bernadette watched him rise unexpectedly from the plush leather chair. He was wearing a gray suit and vest with a faint navy stripe running through it. Knowledgeable in clothes and fashions, Bernadette knew the suit was a very expensive one and had been tailor-made to fit his tall frame. Yet the suit lacked flair. It was three plain, boring, traditional pieces.

Mr. Atwood wasn't old, though he dressed and behaved as if he were. He was thirty. Bernadette knew because his birthdate had come up several times in her work. What a shame, she thought; he looked nothing like a thirty-year-old.

"As you know, Miss Baxter, the holidays are getting closer. Parties and get-togethers will be occurring at every turn."

Bernadette's face brightened. Now this was more to her liking. "Oh yes, my favorite time of the year."

He looked her way with faint relief. "I'm glad to hear this. Then you might be willing to assist me."

Assist him? Was he going to give a party and needed her to be hostess? "What did you have in mind, Mr. Atwood? I'm warning you, without an ounce of conceit, that I'm great with parties."

That quirk of a smile reappeared at the corner of his mouth. "Yes, I'm sure you are, Miss Baxter." Her endless number of friends, mostly male, attributed to that fact, Nicholas thought. "That is why I'm asking you for...help."

"Help?"

Her soft brown eyes stared up at him as if he'd lost his mind. He was wondering the same thing himself. "Er, yes. Some pointers, you might say."

"Pointers?" she echoed again, absently crossing her legs.

The movement brought his gaze to the long shapely line of her calves encased in silky stockings. She was wearing red high heels, he noted. They matched the faint stripe in her tie. She looked quite fetching this morning, but then he realized with a sigh that Miss Baxter always looked fetching.

"I don't really know what else to call them," he said, deliberately shifting his glance from her legs. Two years ago there hadn't been a woman alive who could distract him for any length of time. But now—well, what lay ahead of him was making a shambles of his business-oriented mind.

"Pardon me, Mr. Atwood, but why don't we back up just a bit," she suggested. "I'm afraid I'm not catching any of this."

Sinking back into his chair, Nicholas folded his hands together, then leaned across the wide desk toward his secretary. "Yes, you're right," he agreed briskly. "I'm sure I haven't made myself clear. So, I'll start with . . . the New Year's Eve party."

"You mean the one that Sooner Fidelity gives its executives?"

He nodded, and Bernadette thanked God they were finally beginning to make some progress.

"Yes, that's the one," he replied. "An old colleague in New York is flying down for the party, and he's bringing his sister, Doreen." He looked away from Bernadette's curious gaze to flip through a desk calendar.

"But what has that got to do with me?" Bernadette wondered aloud.

He shook his head as if to ward off her questions. "Doreen and I went to college together back East. She was beautiful, intelligent, enormously popular, and I was quite taken with her. But she never knew I existed."

"Oh!" For a moment it was all Bernadette could manage to say. It was very difficult to imagine Mr. Atwood having a crush on a girl. She also hated the idea of some snobbish girl hurting him. He was such a kind man. He deserved much better.

"I'm sorry it turned out that way for you, Mr. Atwood. Have you seen her lately?"

"What?" he asked, looking confused.

"Doreen. Have you seen her since your college days?" she reiterated.

"Oh, uh, yes, a few times. But it's been a while since the last one. That's why I thought you could help me out before she arrives. You see, they'll be staying with me over the weekend, and I see it as an opportunity to get reacquainted—let her see a different me, so to speak."

Bernadette's brows lifted once again. "You mean you're still interested in this Doreen?"

"Yes, most definitely. I think she could be the right woman for me, even though we don't have much in common."

What a strange thing to say, Bernadette silently mused. Aloud she said, "So now you want to prove to her that you'd be the right man for her?"

Bernadette was shocked by his sudden, brilliant smile. She'd never seen such a transformation!

"That's it exactly, Miss Baxter! I knew you'd understand."

Bernadette didn't fully understand. She'd never associated her boss with a woman before. Still, she was doing her best to grasp the whole picture. "So you want me to give you some pointers on how to entertain her, what she might like, that sort of thing?" Bernadette asked.

"That and a few other things," he answered.

Bernadette smiled reassuringly. "I'd be glad to help out, Mr. Atwood. Of course, you'll have to tell me a little bit about her."

He reached for his coffee, hoping there wasn't a guarded look in his eyes. "Yes, that information would be vital, wouldn't it?" He glanced at her over the rim of his cup. "What are you doing tonight?"

"I—I beg your pardon?" she stammered.

Color crept up over the white collar of his shirt and washed his face. "I mean, if you're not busy tonight, perhaps we could meet and discuss this further?"

Would she even recognize Mr. Atwood out of this office building? she wondered. She'd never pictured him existing out in the humdrum, everyday world.

"Er, well—"

"I could buy your dinner," he quickly suggested. "It's the least I can do for your help."

Dinner with Mr. Atwood? It was an incredible thought. She could imagine what glorious fun Nigel and Joyce could do with that tidbit. But Nigel and Joyce weren't going to know about it, she decided saucily. Neither was Page, who thought she was going to meet him after work for a hamburger.

"Why not?" she said with a smile. "Dinner would be very nice, Mr. Atwood. I only hope that I can be of some help to you with Doreen."

"Oh, I'm certain you will, Miss Baxter. There's no doubt in my mind." He leaned back with a satisfied look on his face.

Bernadette glanced at her watch, which in turn made him look down at the gold one encircling his wrist. "We'd better get busy on the quarterlies, Miss Baxter," he announced. "If you'll get your dictation pad, we'll do as much as we can before lunch."

Bernadette nodded and started out the door. Just as she was thinking it was back to business, he called after her.

"Yes, Mr. Atwood?" she asked, glancing back at him, her hand hesitating on the doorknob.

"You won't discuss this with anyone, will you? I mean, office gossip is never conducive to productiveness in the workplace."

Productiveness in the workplace. It was so like him to bring everything back to business. "I never divulge a confidence, Mr. Atwood. What you and I discuss is strictly our own business," she said with a sassy grin.

With a shaky sigh of relief, Nicholas watched her leave his office. The worst part was over, he thought. Phase one had worked out just as he'd planned. Now it was on to phase two.

Chapter Two

Bernadette found it nearly impossible to concentrate on her work the remainder of the day. Just the idea of her boss being interested in a woman was enough to stun her, but asking Bernadette to help him point Cupid's arrow in the right direction was even more mind-boggling. She had worked closely with the man every day for the past two years, and she'd never dreamed he was secretly pining for some woman in New York! Poor man.

Poor Bernadette, she silently groaned when she realized she had struck the wrong key on the typewriter. How was she possibly going to help Mr. Atwood? Tell him to down about three double Scotches and go after Doreen? The thought made Bernadette giggle furiously under her breath. Nicholas Atwood had probably never been that loose in his life!

A slight tap on the outer door brought Bernadette's head up from the letter she was typing. "Come in," she said easily.

"You're still working?"

Bernadette was surprised to see Page's head poking around the door. Was it that late? She glanced at her watch and realized she'd already worked fifteen minutes past quitting time.

"I didn't realize it was this late," she told him. "I'm just finishing up a letter. Would you like to come in and wait?"

He gave her a cocky grin, then stepped inside. "Where's the boss?" he mouthed silently.

Bernadette nodded to her left. "Still working. It's not unusual for him to stay and work for two or three hours more."

Page jammed his hands into the front pockets of his jeans, which was an incredible feat, considering how tightly the worn denim hugged him. "You don't have to stay, do you? I was looking forward to this evening. There's a rock concert tonight at the Myriad. I thought you might like to go."

"I'd love to—" She broke off suddenly and glanced over the rim of her glasses at her boss's private office. She'd almost forgotten their dinner engagement.

To the majority of women it wouldn't be a matter of choice. How could having dinner with her cool, reserved boss compare to a night of music and sensual fun with the blond hunk standing beside her desk? Still, Bernadette had always had a sense of duty. And Mr. Atwood had been terribly kind to her in the past. It was the least she could do for him. As for Page, well, there was always another time. "But I'm sorry,

Page. I've got to do some extra work for Mr. Atwood tonight.''

"Is the man a slave driver or something? I mean, this is party time, the end of the year and all that. Why don't you ask him to let you off, anyway?'' he asked, giving her a devilish little wink.

She gave him a sweet but pointed smile and pushed her glasses back up on her nose. "Sorry. It's the quarterlies, you see. There's no way I can get around it.''

He shrugged. "If you're sure,'' he drawled. "Then just go ahead and break my heart.''

"Poor Page. I'm sure all the other girls in your little book are already taken,'' she teased while turning her attention back to her typing.

He rested one massive thigh over the corner of her desk and leaned down close to her ear. "None of the girls in my little book look like you do, Berny,'' he purred.

She chuckled under her breath and looked up at him. "Page, you really should change your major to politics. I promise you'll go far—''

"Miss Baxter, have—?''

Mr. Atwood's voice had the same effect as a burst of frigid air. Page instantly stood up while Bernadette fixed her most professional expression on her boss.

"Yes, Mr. Atwood?''

He glanced unaffectedly at Page. It never surprised him to see men in his secretary's office. Her popularity with men was not a secret at Sooner Fidelity and surely not to him. He'd seen many different faces and heard many different names during the last couple of years. "Do you have that letter finished yet? I'd like to get it in the mail this evening before we leave.''

"Yes. I'm just putting the final touches on it." She glanced from him to Page. "Mr. Atwood, this is a friend of mine, Page Sayer. He's OU's newest legend on the football field. Page, this is my boss, Nicholas Atwood. He's executive vice president in charge of sales."

The two men shook hands, with Page saying, "It's nice to meet you, sir."

"My pleasure," Nicholas responded, then turned to Bernadette. "Just bring the letter in when you're finished, Miss Baxter, and I'll sign it."

She nodded and he disappeared into his office as suddenly as he'd appeared. Once he'd shut the door, Page whispered, "How long have you worked for him?"

"Two years. Why?"

Page gave her a baffled look. "And he still calls you Miss Baxter?"

Bernadette rolled the letter out of the typewriter and began to scan it for errors. "Yes. What's so strange about that?" she asked.

Page shrugged. "Rather impersonal, wouldn't you say?"

She lifted her eyes from the letter, then quickly pushed back her chair. "That's just the way Mr. Atwood is—impersonal."

He grinned wickedly as she rose to her feet. "That's good to hear."

"Goodbye, Page," she said wryly. "Sorry about the evening."

He gave her a disappointed look. "Bye, Berny. I'll call you—soon."

She smiled, and he leaned over and kissed her cheek. "You're breaking my heart, you know."

"Don't tell your coach," she whispered and gave him a little wave. Then she hurried into her boss's office.

It was dark by the time Bernadette arrived at her apartment complex in the northwest part of the city.

She lived in a one-bedroom in one of the older blocks of apartments, but it was so well maintained it was almost impossible to determine its age. Bernadette liked the complex because the security was excellent and the landscaping was such that each small yard was exclusive of the others.

"Hi, Berny. Want to play some catch?"

Bernadette turned her head as she climbed out of her Z28 sports car. "Oh hi, Lawrence," she said to the ten-year-old boy standing at the curb by her driveway. "Sorry, I'm in a hurry. I've got a date."

His face wrinkled with a disappointed frown. "Aw, Berny, you've always got a date," he said, shifting his football under the opposite arm. "You might as well get married and get it over with."

She chuckled and started up the walk, with her little blond neighbor beside her. "How can I do that, Lawrence? You're not old enough to get married yet."

He groaned with embarrassment, but there was no mistaking the smile on his face. "So when are you gonna play catch with me? I told Tim you could throw a perfect spiral, and he doesn't believe me. You gotta show him."

She looked down at Lawrence as she unlocked the door. "Well, I guess I'll just have to show him what's what," she said.

"Yeah! When?"

"Soon," she promised, reaching out and ruffling his hair.

"You better," he shot back, already loping back down the concrete drive.

"Hey, Lawrence! Come back here," she called. "I have something for you."

"What is it?" he asked excitedly.

Bernadette went in with Lawrence close on her heels.

"You'll see," she said. "Just a minute and I'll get it." She disappeared down the hall. Lawrence plopped down on a brocade piano stool. He was tossing his football from one hand to the other when she returned to the living room with a slip of paper.

"I got this for you last night. But before I give it to you, you've got to promise to take care of it, okay?"

He nodded seriously. "Okay. But what is it? A coupon for a free burger or one of those frosty desserts?"

"No, nothing related to food." She handed the paper to him, then laughed with glee as his eyes nearly popped.

"Oh, wow! Is this for real, Berny? You're kiddin' me, aren't you?"

"No, Lawrence," she assured him. "Page Sayer really did sign that and especially to you. See, it says To Lawrence. I had a date with him last night, so I asked him to do it for you. Now, am I your buddy, or what?"

"Oh, wow, Berny! This is—wait till I show all my friends. This is really super! Why, once he wins the Heisman, it'll probably be worth money. But I sure won't sell it. Gee, Berny, you're the greatest!" He hopped off the stool, kissed Bernadette on the cheek and ran to the door. "This is the best Christmas present I'll ever get," he insisted. "Thanks, Berny. See you later!"

Bernadette laughed as the door closed behind her little friend. Kids were so special, she thought, and so endearing. She wondered if she would ever have one of her own, then quickly discarded the question. Children meant commitments and responsibilities. At least, that was what they were supposed to mean. She couldn't ever see herself managing anything like that. And there wasn't a man on earth she'd want to get that close to!

Since Mr. Atwood had failed to mention where they'd be eating, Bernadette had no idea what to wear. After much deliberation, she chose a pair of camel-colored slacks and a cream-colored angora sweater with thick shoulder pads and little seed pearls scattered across the bodice. After fingering some mousse through the top and front of her hair, she quickly wound up the back in a tight roll and pinned it in place. The style gave her a fresh, chic image.

She smiled faintly at her reflection as she put on pearl earrings. It was really silly of her to go to any pains with her appearance. This wasn't a date, after all. The smile on her face deepened. Nicholas Atwood on a date with Bernadette? Oh, what a day this had turned into!

The doorbell chimed just as she put down her tube of lipstick. Blotting her lips on tissue paper, she hurried to the door. One glance through the peephole told her it was her boss. She opened the door.

"Good evening, Miss Baxter."

"Good evening, Mr. Atwood. Please come in. I'm almost ready."

He nodded and crossed the threshold into her small but efficient apartment.

"Would you like a drink or something before we go? I have Scotch, vodka, gin, bourbon and a bit of wine," she offered, noting his frown seemed to deepen with each selection.

"Nothing, thank you," he said stiffly. "I rarely drink. I mean, nothing alcoholic, that is."

Bernadette wasn't surprised. "I rarely drink myself," she said honestly. "I just keep it for entertainment purposes."

He folded his hands in front of him. "I can tell. Your complexion is too flawless."

Bernadette looked at him, trying to decide if he was giving her a compliment or merely reporting the result of some scientific study. "Thank you, I guess," she laughed lightly and opened the closet.

He was there to help her on with her coat almost instantly. While he smoothed the material across her shoulders, Bernadette caught the tangy scent of the cologne he always wore. Not for the first time did the choice of his scent surprise her. It was warm, earthy and totally sexy. Not at all in keeping with the cool image he presented.

"Is it snowing outside?" she asked, feeling suddenly very uncomfortable at being alone with Mr. Atwood in her apartment. Which was ridiculous. There couldn't be anyone less harmless than her boss. Still, she had never been around a man like him before, not out of the confines of the office. What should she say to him? How should she behave? Professional, as on the job? Or should she go ahead and relax, let her hair down as she would with anyone else?

Bernadette decided on the latter. If she was supposed to help him snare Doreen's attention, then she had to be herself, right? She hoped he would follow suit and loosen up. It would be one of her first lessons, she decided with a smug sort of pleasure.

"No, it isn't snowing. But it looks very possible. Winter is truly here."

Bernadette picked up her purse from the deacon's bench in the hallway as they headed out the door. "And I love it!" she commented. "There's nothing like snowy weather for snuggling under the covers, watching football and parades on TV on New Year's Day. Or making hot chocolate and greasy, buttery popcorn. Not to mention opening all your packages on Christmas Day."

Nicholas looked at her, wondering how it must be to live as she did, to do the things she did. "You make it sound very different. I always think of it as miserable and slushy with everything looking dead and ugly."

He would, Bernadette thought wryly, looking at his dark-colored, four-door sedan parked by the curb. Its conservative plainness matched his suit and the overcoat he carried on his arm.

"We could take my car," she quickly blurted.

"That's totally unnecessary."

She halted her steps. "Why? Don't you like sports cars?"

He gave the fiery-red, low-slung car on the driveway a cursory glance. "I've never owned one. I really couldn't say."

"Well," Bernadette said with great conviction, "this is just the time for you to drive mine. You might find you'll want to go out tomorrow and trade in your sedan."

Before he could respond, she opened her purse and rummaged for the keys. Mr. Atwood had a stunned expression on his face when she carelessly tossed the keys in his direction. He managed to catch them before they fell on the hood.

"Miss Baxter, I don't think—"

"Believe me, Mr. Atwood, it would please me if you drove my car."

He looked at her as if she were asking him to walk down May Avenue stark naked at high noon. "This is hardly necessary," he said.

Bernadette smiled at him and proceeded to get in the car on the passenger's side. There was nothing left for him to do but follow suit. "I thought you wanted me to give you pointers?" she asked.

He settled himself behind the wheel, then cast her a wary glance. "Pointers? Oh, yes. I did. But what has this car got to do with that?"

"Doreen may like this type of car. Maybe you could feel her brother out about it, or something. Anyway, if she does, you can borrow mine."

Nicholas stared at her keenly from behind his glasses. This was going to involve much more than he'd first anticipated. It was going to be enlightening to say the least, he decided. "I never thought of it," he admitted.

Bernadette smiled to herself and began to show him the essential controls on the dashboard. In a few minutes they were headed down the street.

"So, what do you think?" she asked after he'd driven a while. "Steers like a dream, doesn't it?"

He looked over at her. "It feels like I'm sitting on the ground!" he exclaimed, making her chuckle. "This thing should be on a speedway instead of a city street. It's small and fast and—" he pursed his lips in a negative way "—you could get killed in a thing like this, Miss Baxter!"

Bernadette laughed out loud. "Oh, Mr. Atwood! A person can be killed in any kind of vehicle. And I'm very careful, even when I'm speeding."

His frown deepened, but he didn't reply. "So what do you think?" Bernadette asked. "Would Doreen like to be spirited around the city in something like this?"

Mr. Atwood's thick brows arched above the rim of his glasses as he studied her. "I'm certain of it, Miss Baxter."

It didn't sound as though the idea pleased him, she thought. Then she wondered why he believed Doreen was the woman for him when they had nothing in common. From Bernadette's point of view, the whole thing was really strange. "So you know her pretty well? I mean, well enough to know her taste in things?"

He nodded and turned his gaze back on the traffic. "Very well," he replied. "Much more than she realizes."

Bernadette crossed her legs and glanced at his stern profile. The sight would have chilled a normal person, but Bernadette wasn't put off by it. "The more you can tell me, the more I'll be able to help."

"That's good to know," he said, then asked, "Where would you like to eat?"

Bernadette's expression grew thoughtful. "Where do you think Doreen would like to eat?"

Nicholas frantically searched his mind. "I'd say probably at a pizza parlor. She loves pizza." She certainly sent out for it enough, he thought.

"Mmm. A woman with my kind of taste," she said. "I'll go for that. There's a great place a couple of streets over. Ricetti's. Ever go there?"

He shook his head, and Bernadette looked suddenly contrite. "Oh, I'm sorry, Mr. Atwood. Perhaps you don't like pizza?"

"It's fine," he lied. "And if I'm supposed to be pleasing Doreen, it should be her choice, right?"

"That's very considerate, Mr. Atwood. Not all men are so thoughtful. And I'm sure this Doreen is going to realize in no time at all just what a treasure she has in you."

Her choice of words was enough to choke him. He coughed in earnest as they waited at a red light.

"Are you going to be okay?" she asked with concern.

He nodded and struggled to catch his breath. "Yes, I'm fine. Something just hit me back there."

The light changed as they passed through the intersection. Ricetti's was the next turn on the right. He pulled the Z28 into an empty parking space and killed the motor.

Bernadette brought all her courage to the forefront. Leaning across the seat, she reached for the knot of his tie and began to loosen it.

"What are you doing?" Nicholas gasped. Her touch and nearness shocked him, not to mention the fact that she was loosening a piece of his clothing.

"Don't take it personally, Mr. Atwood, but you just don't look right for driving a sports car and eating at a pizza joint."

By now she'd unbuttoned the collar of his white shirt and pulled down the knot of his tie several inches.

"There. That looks much better," she said decisively.

"You mean, I'm overdressed?" he asked.

Overdressed was an understatement! "Well, a little," she said, trying to be kind but still helpful. "Now take your jacket off and roll up your sleeves."

"My jacket! Miss Baxter, I—it's freezing out there!"

"You'll survive until we get inside," she assured him. "And believe me, women love to see a man's forearms. They do something to us."

The look he shot her was so perplexed it was actually comical. Bernadette had to struggle to keep a straight face.

"I don't really know if I'm ready for all these... lessons," he said, removing his onyx cufflinks and laying them on the dashboard.

"Sure you are. It will be worth it when Doreen falls into your arms," she insisted.

There was absolutely nothing Nicholas could say to that, so he merely did as she suggested.

The pizza place was filled to capacity. It took them a few moments but they finally managed to find a booth in the corner. The air reeked of cigarette smoke and the scent of cheese and spices. On the jukebox in the front of the room, Bruce Springsteen was belting out "Born in the U.S.A."

Bernadette felt right at home. Nicholas was certain he'd just stepped into another dimension, one that closely resembled the Twilight Zone.

They'd barely gotten settled when a waitress came to take their order. There was such a lost look on Mr. Atwood's face that Bernadette took matters into her own hands and ordered for them.

"Isn't that music rather loud?" he asked, half expecting the windows to shatter any moment.

Bernadette shook her head and smiled. "It wouldn't be good if you couldn't feel it, too."

"Feel it?" Nicholas thought music was something a person listened to.

"Yes. The beat, the rock, the motion and drive. And no one can do it any better than the Boss, don't you think?"

"The Boss?" he repeated blankly.

Bernadette motioned her head toward the jukebox. "Bruce. The guy that's singing."

The waitress arrived with their coffee. As he sipped his carefully, Bernadette thought how different he looked with his tie loose and his cuffs rolled back. She'd never seen his arms before. He'd taken his jacket off in the office only a few times. And only because the air-conditioning hadn't been working properly.

She was surprised to note that he had broad shoulders and strong-looking arms, covered with a mat of dark hair. The watch encircling his wrist was a great-looking one, thin and sleek and obviously expensive. The onyx ring on his right hand was nice, too, and Bernadette had a suspicion that underneath it all, Nicholas Atwood was a man with great taste. He was just too afraid to express it.

"Do you eat pizza very often?" she asked.

He shook his head. "I like French food," he said.

"Really? I know nothing about French cooking. But I can do a few Greek dishes."

"You cook?"

She nodded. "When I have the time. I'm not great at it, but I've managed a few dinner parties on my own. Do you cook?"

He looked almost offended by the question. "No, I have someone do my evening meals, or I go out."

She lifted the heavy mug in front of her and sipped the richly brewed coffee. "So, can you tell me a bit about Doreen? How old is she?"

"Her age? I'd say she's in her mid-twenties."

A frown knitted her brows. "That young? I thought you went to college together."

"We did, but she was a freshman and I was a senior."

"Oh, I see," she said. "And what type of person is she? Does she work or have any special interests?"

Nicholas shifted uncomfortably on the padded seat. "She works, but I'm not sure about her interests," he said. Except for one of them, he thought wearily.

"That's going to make it tough," Bernadette mused aloud. "What about her personality? That should tell us something."

He leaned back in the booth. The music had changed to something soft and soulful. Nicholas was amazed to discover he'd already grown accustomed to the loudness. "She's very vibrant, vivacious and outgoing," he said.

No wonder he'd said they had nothing in common, Bernadette thought. If anyone needed a list of antonyms for Nicholas Atwood, he had just given the perfect ones.

"That sounds promising," Bernadette told him. "She probably enjoys doing all sorts of things."

"You're probably right about that."

He didn't offer anything else, and Bernadette wondered if she was going to have to drag it out of him. "Well, let's go on to her looks then. What are they like?"

He cleared his throat. "She's, or at least the last time I saw her, she was very attractive. She's blond, tall and slim, but not too slim. She smiles a lot and has beautiful, white teeth. Her hair is nice, too. She wears it—or she used to," he quickly corrected himself, "wear it long. It's shiny and bouncy, and her eyes crinkle at the corners when she smiles. Sort of like June Allyson, if you know who that is."

"She sounds very nice, Mr. Atwood," she told him. In truth, his description had surprised Bernadette. She'd never expected the woman to be blond or anything else he'd described. She'd been expecting a quiet, studious brunette. So far everything he'd told her resembled herself. What a strange coincidence.

"She is," he agreed in that solemn manner of his. "Very nice."

"Then that gives us all the more reason to put everything into these—er, what shall we call them—lessons?"

He nodded, and she went on with obvious exuberance, "Being a true romantic, I'd feel terrible if we didn't succeed at getting you and Doreen together. And seeing that this is a personal project, would you mind if I spoke frankly?"

Nicholas nodded his permission, yet inside him a strange type of panic threatened to rear its head. Quickly he did his best to squash it down. Panic hadn't made him a vice president for a company like Sooner. And it wouldn't get him what he wanted now.

"I'll put myself in your hands," he managed to say.

She smiled and shook her head. "And that's another thing, would you please not call me Miss Baxter? I'm Berny to all my friends."

"Berny?" he asked in amazement.

"It's short for Bernadette—I've been called Berny since I was ten years old. You see, I wanted to play on the local baseball team, but the women's movement hadn't reached us back then. Still, I had the boys over a barrel 'cause no one could pitch as well as I could. They conceded to my playing as long as I'd pose as a boy so the other teams wouldn't discover the Mets had a girl pitcher. It would have been very embarrassing. You know how boys are. So mother cut my hair off in a pixie cut and I dubbed myself Berny. It worked out great," she added. "We were the area champs that year. Did you play baseball?"

He shook his head, and she asked, "Football?"

"No. I played a bit of soccer. I attended a private school and that was the only sport they offered."

Well, that was a man's sport, she thought. But she certainly couldn't picture Mr. Atwood running up and down a muddy field, getting kicked in the shins, or God help, sweating!

Their pizza arrived and Bernadette savored the smell of tangy Italian sausage emanating from the round pie on the table. She gave him a slice and then served herself.

"My dad always thought it was a shame that I didn't want to be a cheerleader. My mom was one, you see. But I thought it was a waste when I had athletic talent. He changed his mind when I won all-state for basketball though."

"You played basketball?" he asked incredulously.

Bernadette nodded as she swallowed melted cheese and crisp crust. "Forward. My coach was a big man named Al, and he was a real sweetie and a great coach. Took us to state championship four years in a row. We set a record. Goodness, that's been years ago," she said thoughtfully, then glanced across at him. He was staring at her, and she realized she was probably boring him out of his mind.

"Sorry, Mr. Atwood, I'm really running on, and we didn't come here to talk about me. It's just that it's been a while since I thought about that time in my life."

"Everyone likes to reminisce at one time or another," he said. "And since you think I should call you . . . Bernadette, why don't you call me Nicholas?"

"Okay, Nicholas, I'd like that," she said easily and smiled at him.

In spite of himself Nicholas found the pizza delicious. "This is pretty good," he told her. "Maybe I should eat it more often."

"If Doreen likes pizzas this would be the perfect place to bring her," Bernadette suggested. "If she's anything like you described her, I'm sure she'd love it."

His eyelids lowered behind the lenses of his glasses. "Yes, I'm sure she would. I'll keep it in mind."

"You might also keep it in mind to buy her a few Christmas presents. Even though it will be the New Year when you see her, it will let her know you were thinking of her."

"I wouldn't have the faintest idea of what to get her."

Bernadette waved away his words. "Nothing spectacular. Maybe some perfume or an article of clothing. Or some jewelry."

"I've never shopped for a woman," he admitted. "Except for my mother." It was hardly the same. Hardly anywhere near the same!

"Don't worry about it," she assured him. "I haven't finished with all my shopping, so maybe we could go out one day on the weekend and I'll help you choose something."

He hoped the relief he felt didn't show on his face. She was making this much easier than he'd ever expected.

"Thank you, Bernadette, for being so understanding about this. Not many women would look at it the way you are."

"Like I said, Nick, anything to steer true love in the right direction."

Nicholas's attention was suddenly drawn to the fact that she'd called him Nick. No one in his entire life had ever done that. He'd never thought of himself as a Nick, but after hearing Bernadette use the shortened name, he realized he liked it. Nick might not fit his image, but it fit the man inside him.

Bernadette picked up another piece of the thick, hot pizza and bit into it with pure pleasure. After she'd finished chewing, she said, "You know, I'm so glad you're thinking about a woman. I've often thought you needed someone in your life."

He shot her a look that was sort of shocked, sort of wary. "Really? How could you tell?"

She reached for her coffee. "Well, I just meant that everyone needs someone in their life, and I'd never heard you mention anyone before." She shrugged, hoping he didn't think she was getting too personal. He'd already loosened up far more than she'd believed him capable. She didn't want to risk spoiling things by having him retreat into his shell. To be honest, she was enjoying his company, which she hadn't expected at all.

He was so different from all the other men she'd been around. He had a shyness about him that was rather endearing. Bernadette found herself wanting to reach over and squeeze his hand and assure him that he had just as much going for him as anyone else.

"What about you, Bernadette? Do you have someone in your life?"

His question brought a thoughtful look to her face. "Do you mean one single person?" she asked.

Choosing one specific one from all of her male friends was probably too difficult a feat to ask of her, he realized as he waited for her answer.

She shook her head. "Not one certain person. But I have a host of friends I enjoy being with."

"What about that young man in the office today?"

"Page? I've really just gotten to know him," she said. "He's a cutie, isn't he?"

A cutie? Nick could apply a few other adjectives to the man besides that particular one. "More like massive, I'd say."

Bernadette chuckled, then impulsively asked, "Do you have a quarter?"

"You mean like money?"

"What other kind is there?" she teased, then quickly added, "It's for the jukebox. Come on, this is going to be another lesson."

She grabbed him by the hand and pulled him through the crowded tables toward the jukebox. "If Doreen is outgoing, I'm sure she loves music. You need to know what to play," she told him.

"Miss—ah, Bernadette," he protested, "I don't really think I need to know this. She'll only be here a few days."

"It never hurts to know these kinds of things," she insisted. "Once I told a guy I'd like to hear some Righteous Brothers, and he said he didn't own any gospel music. Poor thing, he never knew why I didn't date him anymore."

Nicholas scowled. "You mean you quit dating him just because he didn't know that particular type of music?"

She wrinkled her face at him. "Of course not, Nick! I'm certainly not a snob. It was the fact that he wasn't honest enough to admit that he didn't know something. It showed me what an inflated ego he had, and that is one thing I can't stand."

His sidelong glance at her was thoughtful. "I see what you mean." God, she was talking about honesty and here he was—what was he doing? Digging a deeper hole for himself?

"Okay, now see this guy's name?" she said, pointing to a name listed beneath the colored lights on the jukebox. "Remember it well. Any time you play him you'll know it's always good rock 'n' roll. Now this one," Bernadette went on, "is the one to play if you want to give her something soft and bluesy. Real romance music," she added with a sassy little grin.

In all of his thirty years Nick had never felt as he did at that moment with Bernadette holding his hand, smiling at him as if he were actually dear to her. The quick rush inside him was enough to make him forget where they were and why they were there.

Phase two was working quite well, he decided.

Chapter Three

It had grown very cold by the time they left Ricetti's. A fine mist was falling, some of it already turning to ice on the windshields of the automobiles in the parking lot.

"If this turns into an ice storm, I think I'll take a taxi to work tomorrow morning," Bernadette said, huddling inside her coat while Nicholas started the car.

"It does look like it's going to be nasty. You certainly shouldn't be driving. Why don't you let me pick you up on my way in?"

She didn't know what to say. "Oh, that's too much trouble," she insisted. "A cab is not that expensive."

"It's not really that far out of my way," he said, doing his best to sound casual.

"Where do you live?" she asked, turning around in the seat so she could see him better in the darkness.

He started backing out of the parking space. "Nichols Hills."

The very affluent, long-established part of the city. Bernadette should have known. He probably lived in one of those monstrous old mansions over there. Poor thing, it must be awfully lonely for him, she thought.

"No, that really isn't far away," she admitted, "so I'll take you up on it. Thank you for offering, Nick. And I promise I won't be late."

Her being late for work tomorrow was the last thing on Nick's mind. It was already spinning on to the next two weeks.

When they arrived at Bernadette's apartment, she was struck with the fact that she didn't want the evening to end. Nick's company was proving to be enjoyable. Most men usually made passes at her before the evening got off the ground. It was a relief not to have to ward off advances to get her in the bedroom.

"Would you like to come in for a while?" Bernadette asked as he walked her to the door.

"Do you think—I don't—"

"It's still early, and Doreen will never know," she added teasingly. She unlocked the door and glanced up at him.

He was looking at her in that odd way she'd seen him doing earlier. It was a look she couldn't decipher because she'd never seen it before this evening.

"No, I'm certain she won't know," he acceded after a moment. "And yes, I'd like to come in. If you're sure you want me to."

"I do, or I wouldn't have asked," she said happily.

Her apartment felt blessedly warm after the low temperature outside. Bernadette took Nick's coat and jacket and hung them in the closet along with her coat.

"Why don't we go to the kitchen and make some hot chocolate?" she suggested, turning to find him standing awkwardly in the middle of the living room.

"That sounds fine," he said, following her through an open doorway that led to a tiny dining room and kitchen combination.

A round glass and chrome table stood in front of wide picture windows with heavy drapes, which were open. Out in the distance, Nick could see the lights of the downtown area twinkling like rows of stacked stars. He took a seat at the table while Bernadette filled a saucepan with milk, then flipped on the radio on top of the refrigerator.

It was so different for him to see her in a pair of slacks. She never wore them to work. She was always dressed in soft feminine dresses and skirts, which he admired. He was surprised to find the slacks were just as feminine and equally attractive. Especially the way they clung to her.

"Your apartment is very nice," he said in an attempt to halt his thoughts.

"It's small, but since there's only me, it works out fine. If I want to have a dinner party or something, Mother lets me borrow her house."

"Your parents live here in the city?"

She nodded as she mixed cocoa and sugar in the measuring cup. "My mother lives just a few blocks from here. My dad lives overseas now—France, I believe. He moves around a lot," she explained, unaware of how her face tightened on the last of her words.

The milk was getting warm, so Bernadette slowly stirred in the cocoa. As she stirred, she looked at her boss. "What about you? Are your parents near?"

He shook his head. "Not for a long time. They live on the West Coast now. Mother has a lung problem that forces them to live in a warm climate."

"That's unfortunate. Maybe they enjoy it out there anyway?"

His look was rueful. "Mother would be back in Boston in a second if her health would permit it. California is far too loose and laid-back for her. As far as that goes, so is Oklahoma."

So he knew there was a difference, she thought with some relief. "If your mother is from Boston, how did you ever wind up in Oklahoma?"

The hot chocolate was ready, so she filled two mugs, dropped in some marshmallows and carried them to the table.

"Thank you, Bernadette."

"Be careful," she told him as she took the chair just to his left. "It's very hot."

"Dad is from Oklahoma, but he went to college in New England," he said after taking a cautious sip. "That's when he met my mother. They came back here to live. Dad was a big investor in oil back when Oklahoma was drowning in it."

"I see," she said. "So how did you come to be in insurance?"

He shook his head. "It wasn't a planned thing. I hadn't been back from college very long when the opportunity with Sooner Fidelity presented itself. I'd always planned on being a CPA."

Bernadette's face wrinkled thoughtfully. "Quite a difference, isn't it? Sales executive and CPA?"

"Not really," he said, watching her stir her hot chocolate. "Any kind of business always comes down to facts and figures." He looked at the spoon she'd placed beside his own cup. "Does this spoon have a specific purpose? Am I supposed to be doing something I don't know about?"

Bernadette burst into laughter. "Of course it has a purpose! You either use it to smash the marshmallows down in the milk so they melt, or you scoop up the milk, blow on it and sip it off the spoon."

It was obvious by the look on Nick's face that he didn't know if she was teasing or serious. It was strange how at ease he was with corporate affairs, but how lost in dealing with the simple things in life. "Didn't your mother ever make hot chocolate for you when you were a kid?"

"The only time my mother ever stepped foot in the kitchen was to give the cook the dinner menu." He picked up the spoon and used it to dunk one of the floating marshmallows. "I guess I missed out on the art of drinking hot chocolate."

Among other things, Bernadette thought with a pang of sadness. At least her parents had been fun-loving. They had taught her not only the important, serious side of life, but also how to enjoy the simple things, too. Bernadette had been devastated when her parents had divorced. It had torn the family asunder, and she had known that nothing would ever be the same for any of them. She had hated it! Even now, after all these years, she still hated that it had happened, hated the fact that her daddy lived far away and did not need her mother by his side.

Bernadette's smile was vacant. "I'm sure there's a lot in your life that I've never experienced. Like seeing New England, for instance."

"It's just another part of the United States," he said.

"I hardly think so. It's steeped in history."

"You like history?" he asked with some surprise.

"Yes." She smiled impishly. "But don't tell any of my friends. They'd think I was stuffy. Actually, to be a history teacher was what I first set out to do. But things went off track, and I wound up settling for a short business course."

"Would it be impertinent of me to ask why?"

Bernadette looked at him and realized with a little jolt that he was probably the only person she wouldn't mind telling. "No, of course, it wouldn't. I didn't go on with my studies because, well—my parents divorced when I was eighteen. It was terribly difficult for me to remain in the house and deal with all the changes. It was also hard to support myself and attend college, too. After two years I decided I'd settle for a job and forget about the history."

"I see," he said gently. "So your parents are still divorced?"

She nodded and lifted the mug to her lips. "Very much so," she responded, then determinedly put a smile on her face. "How's the hot chocolate? Not a bad cook, am I?"

He smiled faintly and pushed his glasses up on his nose. "It's quite good."

"Thanks. I only hope my teaching can equal it."

"Teaching?"

"Yes. You know, you and Doreen," she reminded him. "I've got to admit I've never helped a man snare a woman before. I've helped a few girlfriends attract certain guys though, and I'm hoping it will work if I reverse my tactics."

She could see a blush spread on his cheeks. "What's the matter? Did I say something wrong?"

He shook his head. "No. It's—it's just that this is all so embarrassing. I guess you think I'm crazy to ask you about any of this in the first place. But—"

"I don't think you're crazy at all," she said truthfully. "If more men were as open and honest as you're being with me about this, there'd probably be fewer misunderstandings, fewer divorces, fewer broken hearts."

The color on his face deepened, and he suddenly rose from the chair. Bernadette watched him walk over to the windows, where he turned his back to her.

"I—I never was good with girls when I was young," he said pensively. "I never knew how to approach them, what to say to them. When I did say something, it usually came out in a nervous stutter or I would say something so boring they'd simply walk away."

"I think we all have problems like that when we're growing up," she said softly.

"Obviously you grew out of yours," he said.

"I'm sure you have, too. You just don't realize it because you haven't tried again. Am I right?"

He jammed his hands in his trouser pockets. "Maybe. I haven't wanted to try until...until Doreen. She makes me wish I was one of those macho men who know how to flirt and flatter and all the other things women like."

He must be crazy about the woman! Bernadette couldn't imagine any of the men she'd dated agonizing over her this way. No, they all seemed confident, arrogant—macho. It almost made her wish they were more like Nick. A little bit of agonizing would be nice, wouldn't it?

"All women aren't that keen on macho men," she tried to assure him.

He looked at her and frowned. "Doreen is." She was always surrounded by macho men, he acknowledged to himself. She had to be more than keen on them.

"How can you be sure of that? Some women say one thing and mean something altogether different." Good Lord, she wasn't doing much for the female race with that line, but at the moment she felt Nick's ego was more important.

"I'm sure," he said. "She's always—I—her brother tells me about the guys she dates."

Well, that only meant she'd help him that much harder. "Okay, what makes you think you're not macho enough for Doreen?" she asked him.

His eyes widened on her, then he glanced down at himself. "I'm not totally blind, Bernadette. I know I don't look like . . . like some of the men you know."

Bernadette noted the doomed expression on his face, then looked at him, really looked at him. No, he wasn't a heavily muscled jock, but still . . . Her eyes followed the lines of his shoulders and chest, his lean waist and long legs. If she stripped off his clothes she'd bet anything he'd look—good.

Berny! What are you thinking about? You've worked with the man for the past two years, you've hardly given him a second glance and now you're suddenly wanting to strip him? But she hadn't known him, she defended her thoughts, and now she was beginning to.

"Macho is just a word, an impression," she hastily assured him. "All you need is to—" Abruptly she rose from the chair and walked over to him. "Do you really need these glasses?"

Before Nick could answer she reached up and pulled them from his face. A pair of brilliant blue eyes stared back at her. Bernadette was stunned at the difference it made in his looks. His eyes were actually sexy!

"Bernadette! I can't see without them!"

"Oh Nick, you look, you look great! We simply must get you down to the mall and purchase contact lenses for you."

"Contact lenses!" he sputtered.

Bernadette glanced at her wristwatch. "Darn it! It's too late. They're just closing." She glanced back up at him. "I know, we'll go tomorrow on our lunch break. I know a great place where I buy my reading glasses."

"Bernadette, this is going too far!"

"Nick, I had the impression you'd do most anything for this woman."

He looked as though he were about to protest, but instead he grimaced and asked, "Does it really make a difference?"

She gave him one of her dazzling smiles. "It's going to work miracles, believe me, Nick. Hasn't any woman told you what gorgeous eyes you have? Why have you been hiding them?"

"Hiding them?" he repeated the question with surprise. "I thought I'd merely been trying not to be blind."

Reluctantly she put the glasses back on his face. "Well, that's important, I agree. But in this case we're waging an all-out campaign for Doreen."

He gave her another one of those odd looks, and Bernadette dropped her hands from his face.

"But contact lenses," he protested. "Aren't they difficult to wear? My eyes will look all bloodshot and—"

"They have these new soft kind now that you can keep in almost indefinitely." Excited and pleased that she'd thought of the idea, she squeezed his hand with encouragement. "It'll be worth it. I promise."

How could he possibly think about contact lenses with her standing so near? Her fingers had touched his face, and when she'd raised her arms to put his glasses back on, her breasts had brushed against him. He still wasn't quite sure he was breathing.

"Is something wrong? Am I going too fast for you?"

He cleared his throat and reached up to adjust his glasses. "Er, no, Bernadette," he said.

"Well, just tell me if I am. A loud 'Shut up' will do it."

The corner of his mouth moved into a faint smile. "I'll remember that," he told her. "But for now I really must be getting home. I want to look over that report we finished this afternoon."

"But you haven't finished your hot chocolate," she said, stepping away from him.

"I—it was very good, but I'm still full of pizza," he explained.

Seeing he was intent on leaving, Bernadette led the way back to the living room, collected his jacket and coat from the closet and handed them to him. She was really disappointed that he was going. And that surprised her a great deal. She said, "I'm sorry you have to leave, Nick. I've really enjoyed the evening."

He studied her closely. Had she really enjoyed it? "I'm glad," he murmured.

Impulsively she leaned over and kissed his cheek. "Thank you for such nice company," she said softly.

Nick's nostrils flared as her sweet scent rushed to his head. Her lips were soft, so soft. How would they taste beneath his? The thought caused him to almost stumble as he backed away from her.

"I'll pick you up in the morning, as we planned," he told her, grabbing the doorknob.

Confused, Bernadette watched him back out of the door. "It's very sweet of you, Nick. I'll be ready," she assured him.

What was the matter with him? she wondered. He was acting as though he couldn't get away from her fast enough. Had she said or done something to offend him?

"Good night," she called to his retreating figure.

He turned and gave her a stiff wave, then went on to his car. Bernadette closed the door, automatically locking it.

What a strange day, and how different that Nicholas Atwood was from the man she'd worked with for the past two years. It had been very pleasant seeing this other side of him. She was even happy that he thought so much of her that he chose her to help with his problem.

Doreen. Bernadette rolled the name over her tongue and wondered why it seemed so distasteful. The unknown woman better prove to be worthy of Nick. He deserved the best, and Bernadette was going to make sure he got it.

The following morning, the streets showed only patches of ice. Bernadette could have driven herself to work, but she felt it would have made her appear ungrateful to call Nick and tell him so. Therefore, she was standing out on the drive waiting for him when his dark green sedan pulled up at the curb.

He got out quickly and put a hand on her arm. "Careful," he said. "The ice is slick."

As Nick helped her into the car, Bernadette thought it was the first time he'd ever touched her of his own initiative. For some unexplainable reason she was acutely conscious of his fingers. They left a warm imprint even after he released her.

"Good morning, Nick," she said once they were both settled inside his car. "Did you have a restful night?"

Nick watched her smooth the wrinkles out of her woolen skirt. It was red and green plaid and her sweater was a matching green. She looked very bright and Christmassy and his spirits soared. This was the first time ever that he was looking forward to the holidays.

"Very good, thank you," he responded. "And you?"

"I slept like a log. Did you find anything wrong with the report?"

Report? All he'd managed to do once he got home was sit on the couch and stare off into space. The report had lain untouched on his desk. He was losing his grip, of that much Nick was certain. "I'm afraid I didn't get to it," he said brusquely. "I'll do that this morning after we go over the correspondence."

"Did you have breakfast?" She glanced at him. He was dressed in another dark, three-piece suit. His tie was equally dark and conventionally striped. Bernadette decided that something would have to be done about his clothes before Doreen arrived in the city. But for right now she would settle for the contact lenses. Smiling to herself, she imagined what her co-workers would say when they saw him without his thick glasses.

"I never eat breakfast."

"Shame on you, Nick!"

"You're a big breakfast-eater?" he asked.

"I always stop at Maria's," she told him. "Would you care to join me? The pastries are delicious. So is the coffee."

Join her for breakfast? It amazed Nick how successful his plan was turning out to be. But why shouldn't it be successful? he thought. He was a brilliant businessman, and his business was selling. This was no different than any other corporate challenge he'd faced. You plied the buyer with an offer he couldn't refuse, then sat back and reaped the benefits. He said, "I wouldn't want to impose."

She smiled at him. "Nonsense. Joyce doesn't mind having extra company."

"Joyce?"

Bernadette nodded. "Joyce Knight. She works in data. Short, dark-haired. Do you recall her?"

He shook his head. "Sorry, there's so many people in data. And I don't really know that many Sooner employees, except the—"

"Executives," she finished for him. "I should have realized that."

How snobbish that made him sound, he thought dismally. But it wasn't really that way. He just wasn't that good a mixer. Therefore, he mixed only with those he was forced to associate with.

When they arrived at Maria's, it was as crowded as usual. The warm, yeasty smell of hot bread, mingled with the aroma of spices and freshly brewed coffee, filled the little shop.

Bernadette took Nick by the hand and led him through the crowded tables. Several people spoke to her along the way. Most of them were businessmen who watched for her arrival every morning. Bernadette was unaware that her legs were a hot item discussed among them. They'd been looking forward to a miniskirt this morning. The long plaid covering her knee-high boots was a disappointment to the men, but not nearly as much as seeing Nicholas Atwood as her companion.

Joyce was in a corner table by a window. She waved when she saw Bernadette, then her jaw dropped when she noticed who Bernadette had in tow.

Bernadette hoped that Joyce had the good sense to act casual once they got to the table.

"Good morning, Joyce. Do you know Nick, my boss?" Of course she knew him! Everyone who worked at Sooner Fidelity knew the rich wizard in the business world.

"Er, uh, no, I don't believe we've met properly. But your reputation precedes you, Mr. Atwood."

His face took on a faint frown, and Bernadette wanted to kick Joyce's shins beneath the table.

"It's nice meeting you, Joyce," Nick said, then glanced at Bernadette to see if she was ready to be seated.

The table was very small, making the chairs extremely close together. Once he'd taken his own seat, his shoulder was practically pressing against Bernadette's.

A waitress appeared in the crowd. Bernadette caught her attention and the woman worked her way over to their table.

Bernadette looked over to Nick. "What would you like, Nick?"

"Plain glazed will be fine," he answered, "and a coffee."

Bernadette opened her mouth. She badly wanted to remind him this was a pastry house and ordering plain glazed was like ordering a hamburger at a steak house. But she didn't. He probably already thought she was bossy and pushy, and she didn't want to reinforce that. She just wanted him to see and taste and feel everything she did and enjoy it all as much as she did.

Knowing Joyce was darting curious glances from her to Nick, Bernadette dragged her eyes away from him and looked up to the waitress. "Two plain glazed, one of those peanut things, an apple fritter and two coffees."

"This place must be very popular," Nick said surveying the crowded room after the waitress had left. "Do you come here often?"

"Every morning," Bernadette answered. "I suppose by now I'm hooked on the sugar and caffeine."

He smiled at her. She was so warm and lovely, and the red lipstick she was wearing made it difficult to keep his eyes off her mouth. Memory of her kiss flooded his mind.

"There was a bit of ice over my way," Joyce spoke. "How 'bout you, Berny?"

"I collected Bernadette this morning so she wouldn't have to drive on it," Nick told her.

Joyce's mouth parted with stunned idiocy. Bernadette wondered if Nick would notice if she stomped Joyce's toes beneath the table.

"I always ride the city bus," Joyce finally said. "It's dependable and cheap."

He nodded and looked around again. There were a couple of men he recognized from Sooner Fidelity. They were both junior executives. He wondered if they'd noticed his being with Bernadette. It would be miraculous if they hadn't. He was certain every male eye in the house had been on Bernadette when they walked through the door. Talk about the two of them would be running rampant, but why should he care? He knew there were always innuendos flying around about himself and his sexy secretary.

The waitress brought their orders, and Bernadette bit into hers with delicate relish. Nick sipped his coffee and struggled to ignore the pressure of Bernadette's thigh against his.

"Have you finished your Christmas shopping yet, Joyce?" Bernadette asked.

"Almost. I can't decide whether to get my ex something or not."

"Does he get you something?"

Joyce grimaced. "Usually."

"Then I think you should get him something. After all, you did part on amicable terms," Bernadette reminded her.

"Maybe you're right," Joyce decided. "How about you, Berny? Have you finished your shopping?"

Bernadette shook her head as she chewed a piece of the apple fritter. "No. I still need to get something for both my parents." She glanced at Nick. "And Nick and I have a little shopping to do, don't we?"

His brows lifted above the rim of his glasses. She'd promised not to tell anyone about this whole thing. Was she already breaking her word?

"Er, uh, yes, we do," he said reluctantly.

"Oh, really?" Joyce asked curiously.

Bernadette winked conspiratorially at Nick. "Yes. Nick wants me to help him pick out gifts for the other Sooner executives." Which was the truth, she thought. Whiskey for some, cigars for others. It was a job she'd always done for him when holidays came about. "Frankly, I believe they should give Nick a double bonus for his Christmas gift this year. Sales have shot forward this year."

"Bernadette," he protested lightly. "That's my job—to make sales go up. I didn't do anything spectacular."

She placed her hand on his forearm and reached for her coffee cup with the other. "Nick, don't be so modest. Besides, I'm your secretary. I should be allowed to brag about my boss. I think you've worked miracles this year. Sales are up fifty percent. No one else can boast that kind of record, especially in this sluggish economy."

No one ever praised him as Bernadette did, and it never failed to touch Nick. As far back as his early childhood it had been evident to his parents and teachers that he had a brilliant mind. Therefore his success had not been praised or encouraged—it had been expected. Now that he was a successful businessman it was expected even more. His family, his friends and fellow executives looked at him and expected nothing but the best from him at whatever he did. He wasn't paid to fall short, they all said. But not

Bernadette. He felt himself smiling at her. "We have done a good job this year, haven't we, Berny?"

Bernadette's face virtually glowed back at him. Nicholas Atwood rarely handed out praise, so she knew it wasn't given lightly. She'd worked her tail off for him these past two years. But he knew it and he appreciated it. That made it all worthwhile to Bernadette.

"Yes, we have," she murmured in agreement.

Across the table Joyce was examining the look Berny and Nicholas Atwood were exchanging. It was anything but boss-secretary. "I heard the Christmas party was going to be the twenty-fourth. Apparently Sooner has made profits this year. We're going to have a band, dancing and catered food."

Bernadette's eyes widened at this news. "Really? Nick, this is going to be great. You will be there, won't you?"

"I'll stick my head in long enough to wish the employees a Merry Christmas. But that's about all," he said.

"Nick," she protested. "There'll be dancing and fun." She lowered her voice, darting Joyce a wary glance. "It'll be a good opportunity for us to, well, you know."

Knowing Joyce was staring at them openly, Nick pulled his eyes away from Bernadette, cleared his throat and reached for his coffee.

"Yes, well, you might be right, Berny. We'll discuss it before the twenty-fourth gets here."

Pleased that he hadn't turned down her suggestion, Bernadette smiled at him, then looked across to Joyce. "I take it you'll be going, too?"

Joyce looked from Nicholas Atwood to Bernadette, then gave Bernadette a pointed smile. "I wouldn't miss it for the world."

Chapter Four

Bernadette was typing, her mind in deep concentration, when a slight tap sounded on the office door. Before she could say come in, Nigel sauntered in and made himself at home on the corner of her desk.

"My, my. What a busy little girl you are these days," he drawled.

Bernadette looked up at him over the rim of her glasses. "Is this visit business or just a plan to ruin my day?" she asked dryly.

He chuckled at her question. "I heard you turned down Page last night."

"Really? How did you manage that?"

"I ran into him in the corridor as I was leaving. The boy was nearly in tears. It's a shame what you do to the male race, Berny."

"It's really a shame what I'd like to do to you, Nigel," she retorted.

Grinning broadly, he leaned closer to her face. "I'm ready whenever you are," he invited in a shameless voice.

"Nigel," she warned, pushing her chair back away from him and the desk.

Frowning good-naturedly, he straightened up to a sitting position. "I heard you and the wizard had breakfast together at Maria's," he commented.

Her eyes dared him to make something of it. "Mr. Atwood was kind enough to drive me to work this morning."

"Mr. Atwood," he mouthed silently, then said aloud, "I thought Joyce said you were calling him Nick?"

Bernadette pushed her glasses up on her nose and deliberately turned back to her work. "You two make me tired. The only thing you're good at around here is gossiping. You're always trying to dig up something. And if you can't find anything, then you just make it up."

"Now really, Berny, I wouldn't go so far as to say that," he quickly defended himself.

"For your information—" she began tartly, but was interrupted by the buzz of the intercom on her desk. "Yes, Nick?" she answered.

"Berny," Nick's voice sounded back, "did you happen to find my cufflinks in your car? I left them on the dashboard last night, remember?"

Bernadette glanced up at Nigel. The astonishment on his face was monumental.

"Er, no, I didn't. But I'm sure they're still there," she spoke into the intercom.

"I hope so. They were rather expensive. I'm usually not so negligent," he said. "But after we—well, by the time I left your place I'd forgotten about them."

"I—please don't worry about it, Nick. I'm sure I'll find them when I go home."

"Thank you, Berny."

The intercom went silent. Bernadette refused to look at Nigel. She picked up the report she'd been working on and started to proof her typing.

"Well, now, isn't that enlightening?" Nigel purred.

"It's not what you think," Bernadette snapped.

Nigel clucked his tongue and slid off the corner of the desk. "Poor Page thrown over for—"

"Don't say anything, Nigel," Bernadette interrupted angrily. She never minded the other employees gossiping about her; she took it all with a grain of salt. But she would *not* stand for anyone thinking or speaking wrongly of Nick. He didn't deserve it. But what could she say? How could she get around this without breaking her promise to Nick?

"And so defensive, too," he added tauntingly. "Wonder of wonders."

"Nigel, if you don't have any business reason for being here, then get out. I'm very busy," she said coldly.

He must have seen that he'd thoroughly angered her because he said, "As a matter of fact, I do need some information on the Rockwell account."

Bernadette quickly crossed to the file drawers and took out the folder. "See that it's returned to me in the same shape it left this office," she said, slapping it into his hand.

Nigel chuckled as he waltzed out the door.

Thirty minutes later, Bernadette tapped on Nick's door and entered his office. Several files were spread across his desk, but he wasn't working. Again his chair was turned toward the wall of glass facing downtown Oklahoma City. His hands were linked at the back of his dark head. It was obvious to Bernadette that he was miles away.

"Nick, it's lunchtime. I thought we might drive over to the mall," she said.

At the sound of her voice, he quickly turned. There was still a thoughtful look on his face. Probably thinking of Doreen, she concluded. Bernadette wondered what it would be like to have a man adore her that much. True, she had lots of dates. Men were drawn to her because of her looks, but Bernadette had never experienced love. Nor had she been loved in return. Maybe Joyce was right. Maybe Bernadette did deliberately change the men in her life quickly so that they wouldn't get a chance to fall in love with her.

"I didn't realize it was that late," he said with a glance at his watch.

"You haven't changed your mind about the contacts, have you?"

He rose from his chair as Bernadette moved farther into the room. "I suppose not. Since you think it's so important."

She folded her hands in front of her. He seemed down. Bernadette hoped it wasn't about something she'd done or said. "Well, if I were Doreen, I'd be just as impressed with you wearing glasses."

"That's very sweet of you to say, Berny," he said, his face suddenly brightening.

She smiled at him as he fetched his overcoat from the closet. "You must remember that I know what's behind those glasses. But I'm not the important one here. Doreen is."

Nicholas tossed the coat over his arm, then shut the closet door. "Berny," he said with a grimace, "I think . . . there's something I should tell you."

He crossed the room to join her and Bernadette looked anxiously up at him.

"Oh, is something wrong? Has Doreen backed out on making the trip?"

Nick studied her sweet face and was suddenly overwhelmed at her kindness, her eagerness to help him. No one had ever shown Nicholas Atwood that before.

"No, it's just that I . . ."

"Yes?"

He shook his head and sighed. "I think I should tell you that it's been ages since I last danced."

Bernadette got the impression that hadn't been what he'd first started to tell her. "You're referring to the Christmas party?"

He nodded, then frowned. "I don't want to seem ungrateful to you, Berny. But dancing—well, that's just not me."

"How do you know it isn't?"

"I went to a few dances my fraternity held. They were memorable, but for all the wrong reasons," he said. Then he opened the door and stood aside to allow her to go before him.

As they passed through Bernadette's work space, she reached for her fur coat. Nick was there almost instantly taking the garment from her and helping her into it.

"Can you dance?" she hazarded the question.

He ushered her through the outer door and into the wide corridor. "A bit of the ole one-two-one-two. But that's about it."

"Well, that's all you need to know," she quickly assured him.

He glanced down at her as they walked toward the elevator doors. "I have a feeling Doreen knows much more than that about dancing."

"And you don't want to disappoint her," Bernadette reasoned as he pushed the down button on the wall.

The doors swished open and the two of them stepped into the cage to join several other people. Bernadette didn't recognize any of them, and since none of them acknowledged Nick, she took it that he didn't know them, either.

"So what kind of music will be at the New Year's Eve bash?" she asked.

"In the past it's always been a wide range of popular music."

"Well, that sounds safe enough. Surely there will be some slow selections so that you can ask her to dance."

Nick rubbed his jaw. This was getting worse by the minute. He was quickly learning it was true what they said about lying. Once one was told, it just seemed to call for more.

"Berny, I—let's just forget this whole thing about the Christmas party. It's very nice of you to want me to be there, but to be honest, I'm very uncomfortable at parties. I'm not a partying, dancing, whooping-it-up kind of guy."

"That's all the more reason you should go," she said brightly. Impulsively she linked her arm in his and gave it a little squeeze. "Look, Nick, you don't have to be a great dancer or a marvelous conversationalist to enjoy a party. Just be yourself and it'll all turn out well."

He looked at her smiling face and felt the urge to groan aloud. What had ever possessed him to start all this in the first place? The feel of Bernadette's arm on his answered the question for him.

They took Nick's sedan to the shopping mall. Behind the wheel he seemed very quiet and pensive. Bernadette took his silence as worry.

"Look, Nick," she spoke up after they'd traveled a few blocks in the busy lunch-hour traffic, "since you're so worried about this dancing business, I've got a great idea."

His eyes left the street just long enough to glance her way. "What kind of idea?"

She shifted around in the seat to face him and looked at him with enthusiasm. "I want you to come over tonight."

"Come over," he repeated confusedly as though she'd just spoken in a foreign language. "Tonight?"

"Yes, tonight. I thought we might do a little dancing."

He gaped at Bernadette, then stomped on the brake when he realized the car in front of him had come to a halt. The tires squealed against the pavement for several feet before stopping, with the bumper just a few inches from the Cadillac in front of them. Nick let out a relieved sigh and watched the nose of his car continue to sway up and down from the abrupt stop.

Bernadette went on as if she were perfectly accustomed to near traffic mishaps. "I've got a wonderful stereo system and a stack of LPs. It will get you practised and limbered up before Doreen gets here," she told him.

The traffic began to inch forward once again. Nick warily stepped on the accelerator.

When Doreen gets here, his mind repeated the words. At the time Nick had first considered this whole thing, he'd refused to consider what would happen when New Year's Eve finally did arrive. He figured it would all be worked out by then. Now he wasn't quite so sure.

"I couldn't ask it of you," he said. "You've already been so kind."

She waved away his words. "Nonsense, I love to dance. And why don't you come early? I'll fix us a hot dog, or taco or something."

Even now he could see the headlines. Big Hypocrite Nicholas Atwood Uncovered at Sooner Fidelity Bash. "I never realized there'd be so much involved in all this," he admitted.

She chuckled and crossed her legs. "You just didn't realize what a thorough teacher I'd be."

His smile was hesitant but still there, Bernadette noticed. It made her happy to see it.

"No, I guess I didn't," he told her.

Fortunately the optical place wasn't busy and Nick was quickly ushered into an examining room. However, by the time the optometrist had examined Nick and they had discussed the transition to contact lenses, their lunch hour had passed.

"I'm sorry, Nick," Bernadette apologized as they were walking back to the car.

"Don't worry about it. You're forgetting you're out with the boss."

Her brows lifted in surprise. She'd never expected Nicholas Atwood to say something like that. He was always so punctual, so proper. She supposed people, including herself, had always misjudged him.

"That's right," she said, smiling brightly at him. "And I'm starving."

"Starving after all those pastries. I didn't know you ate so much."

They had reached the car and Bernadette chuckled as he opened the door for her. "It's really unladylike, isn't it?"

"I'd say it's more like incredible," he said. "I can remember my mother eating like a bird to keep her weight down."

After he'd taken his place behind the wheel, Bernadette said, "I get a lot of physical exercise after working hours. It helps burn up all those calories. What about you, Nick?"

He looked over at her as the engine sprung to life. He seriously doubted their exercise regimens involved the same thing. "I go to the gym when I have the chance. Sometimes I cycle for long distances on the weekend."

He backed out of the parking area and maneuvered the car onto the busy thoroughfare.

"You mean biking?" Bernadette asked curiously.

He nodded, and she said in an eager voice, "I have a bike, too! But I can rarely find anyone to ride with me. Maybe we could—" Her smile fading, she stopped and shook her head. "I keep forgetting about Doreen. If things work out for you, you'll be spending all your time with her."

"Well, maybe not all my time."

Bernadette shot him a puzzled look and he quickly went on, "I mean, Doreen lives on the East Coast. I couldn't possibly spend all my time with her." He kept his eyes on the heavy traffic.

Bernadette studied him with a perplexed expression. "But I thought that was the whole idea behind this—your making a play for Doreen. Aren't you going to ask her to stay here in the city?"

Nick frowned. "Berny, you're expecting miracles from me if you expect Doreen to suddenly uproot herself and stay here for me."

She sighed and said, "Well, most women are willing to follow the man they love. I would be." Why had she told him that, Bernadette wondered. Two or three months' attention was all she ever gave any man. Now here she was telling Nick she'd be willing to follow one halfway across the continent. She was really reacting strangely to her boss.

"But you're forgetting, Berny. Doreen doesn't love me."

"Not yet," Bernadette countered, "but I have no doubt that she will."

In spite of it all, Nicholas had to smile at her. He didn't know why she had such confidence in him, but it gave him an immense feeling he couldn't quite describe. He only knew it felt wonderful.

They stopped at a small restaurant on their way back to the office and had a pleasant meal. It was a place Nick often frequented. Even though it was busy, the service, along with the food, was exceptional. It was a far more expensive lunch than Bernadette could afford, but she hardly had to worry about it. Nick refused to let her pay her share.

Bernadette was very busy for the remainder of the afternoon. The sales information she typed up was one of the most important parts of the reports issued to the stockholders at the end of the year. It was long and involved and contained an endless list of numbers, which made it more difficult to type.

Nick received several phone calls, one from a big company he was negotiating a sale with. It would mean an enormous profit for Sooner Fidelity, and Bernadette knew that Nick had worked long and hard and had done a bit of brilliant maneuvering to convince the customers to put their trust in Sooner.

That wasn't surprising to Bernadette. Nick was a man who invariably gained a person's trust. He had an honest, intelligent air about him that was not a practised thing. It dawned on Bernadette that Nick was one of the very few men that she trusted to be totally honest with her.

At three-thirty he strode into her office with several folders tucked beneath his arm. She looked up questioningly at him.

"A board meeting has been called. It'll probably run until five," he explained.

"Any messages that I think are important, I'll leave on your desk," she assured him.

He reached for the doorknob, then glanced back at her. "And don't worry about working overtime on the report. As long as we have it ready to go out by the twenty-third we'll be in fine shape."

"Thank you, Nick. Shall I look for you around six-thirty, or seven?"

It was amazing how fresh and vibrant she looked even though it was nearing the end of the day. Especially since she was the most thorough, hard-working secretary he'd ever had. It galled him that his fellow executives had made sly insinuations that Nicholas had hired Bernadette because of her looks. He didn't care how many cutting labels they applied to him, but he wouldn't stand for anything said wrongly against Bernadette. It was very undeserving.

"Yes, I'm looking forward to it, Berny," he said, then shocked her with a warm smile.

"I'm sorry, Page, but I've got an engagement with my boss tonight. There's no way I'll break it," Bernadette spoke into the telephone.

She'd just gotten into her apartment and began shedding her clothes when the telephone had rung. The massive running back wanted to take her to dinner. But Bernadette just couldn't imagine breaking the invitation she'd extended to Nick. Even more than that, she realized she didn't want to break it. She could talk to Nick about things a person like Page would find completely boring. And with Page, all she would hear about was the upcoming Orange Bowl game.

"I didn't realize your boss required so much of your free time," he countered dryly.

"This is something special," she said. "Perhaps we can have dinner another time?"

He sighed. "I'd be crazy not to give you a rain check, Berny," he told her. "And I won't let you off the hook so easily next time."

"Goodbye, Page," she said and hung up before he had the chance to continue the conversation.

Bernadette knew that Joyce and a few of her other girlfriends would think she was crazy for turning down Page Sayer. But Bernadette had never been typical.

She had worked closely with Nicholas Atwood for the past two years. He'd been exceedingly kind and generous, but he'd always been strictly business. She'd never had an inkling of what he was like as a person outside the office. It was very enjoyable getting this chance to know him better. It made working for him just that much more pleasurable.

Before she went to the kitchen, Bernadette changed into a pair of tight jeans and a white sweatshirt and pulled her hair back into a ponytail. By six-thirty she had heated wieners, buns and thick spicy chili. French fries were sizzling in the deep fryer and the glass table was set for two.

The doorbell rang just as she started to test the potatoes for doneness. She ran to the front door and quickly ushered Nick in out of the cold.

"Come on into the kitchen, Nick. My potatoes are about to burn."

Nick opened his mouth to say hello, but before he could get it out he found himself watching her backside fly toward the kitchen. Smiling to himself, he followed at a slower pace.

The kitchen was cozy and very warm. Bernadette was dumping French fries into a woven basket lined with a paper towel. He couldn't ever remember a woman cooking for him, and he wondered why Bernadette doing so seemed so natural to him.

"It smells good in here."

Smiling, Bernadette turned at the sound of his voice. Her mouth promptly fell open when she saw him removing his leather jacket.

"Is something wrong?" he asked.

"Uh, no," she quickly assured him. "It's just your clothes. You look . . . great." And he did, she thought with surprise. He was wearing khaki trousers with a white, long-sleeved polo shirt tucked in at his trim waist. It was amazing how different he looked out of those austere, three-piece business suits.

He placed the short, tobacco-brown jacket over one of the dining room chairs. "I remembered you'd said I was overdressed last night. I didn't want to make the same mistake twice."

Bernadette felt herself blushing, something she hadn't done in a long time. She really wasn't quite sure why she was doing it now.

"I—forgive me for staring—I just never thought you wore casual clothes. I mean, I've always seen you in just a suit." She shook her head and laughed self-consciously. "You really look nice, Nick. Not at all like my boss."

He smiled crookedly, then said, "I don't feel like your boss."

There was a soft inflection in his voice. Bernadette was distracted by it and his words. It was almost as if he were implying that he thought of her as a woman. But that was a silly idea. He wanted Doreen, not her.

"Why don't you go ahead and take a seat, Nick? Everything's ready. All I have to do is carry it over to the table."

"Here, let me help you," he told her. "I don't know anything about cooking, but at least I can carry."

Bernadette handed him the French fries, then contended with the hot dishes holding the wieners and chili. In just a few moments they had everything on the table and Bernadette was filling a couple of tumblers with ice and soft drinks.

"Are you excited about getting your contacts tomorrow?" she asked him as she took a seat to his left.

"I'm wondering what it's going to be like without glasses," he confessed. "I've worn them since I was a small boy. I'll probably feel naked without them."

"Or maybe a little self-conscious?"

His brows lifted. "Berny, I think you realize things about me before I realize them myself."

She shrugged. "Just a simple deduction. I imagine anyone would feel self-conscious after wearing glasses for that long. I hope you're not doing it just because I suggested it. I want you to do it for yourself." Maybe she should have added "and for Doreen, too," but she wasn't going to. She'd had time to think about this whole thing and she knew she wanted to help Nick because she liked him and wanted him to be happy. She certainly wasn't doing it for some woman she'd never even seen before.

His smile was full-fledged as she passed him a warm hot dog bun. "Believe me, Berny, I'm doing it for the right reasons."

The right reasons. He must mean catching Doreen's eye. Why did she suddenly have the urge to let out a flat sigh? "I'm really looking forward to the Christmas Eve party. You know, this is the first time the company has gone to this much expense for its employees. It must be due to all those sales you made this year."

His mouth twisted wryly. "Insurance sells itself, Bernadette. Just like people sell themselves to other people."

"Pooh! There's thousands of insurance companies across the United States. You've got to know when, how, and just what to offer," she countered. She dipped a knife in the mustard jar and began to spread the condiment over her bun. "Is that what you're trying to do with Doreen? Sell yourself to her?"

She could see his blue eyes widen behind his glasses. "No. Not really. I just want her to see me as I really am, and dispel the impression she has of me."

"Oh. What kind of impression does she have?" Bernadette asked curiously.

He shrugged a shoulder. Bernadette's gaze was drawn once again to his clothes. The knit shirt showed off the broadness of his shoulders and his muscular chest. Now that he wasn't hidden beneath all that drab material, she could see he had a nice, very fit body.

"Bookwormish. No. Maybe not that, maybe more like a business machine that does its job very well, but nothing outside of that."

"Nick," she protested, "that sounds awful."

"But true," he said.

"How can you know that?"

Bernadette passed him the French fries. He took them, saying, "It must be what she thinks. She never looked at me as a man."

"Perhaps that's because you didn't let her know you were interested in her as a man?"

He shot her a strange look.

"Nick, you *have* let her know you're interested, haven't you?"

He shook his head.

"When do you plan on telling her?" she asked, bewildered.

"I've been thinking about that a lot these past couple of days. And I've come to the conclusion that the time has to be just right."

Nicholas watched her tongue slip out and lick the salt and ketchup from her upper lip. "I—I believe at the New Year's Eve party. I can't foresee telling her anytime sooner.''

"But don't you think you'll be wasting precious time? Don't you think you should tell her before then?''

Bernadette watched him dollop chili onto his hot dog. Not for the first time did his behavior seem odd to her, but then she had to step back and tell herself that there was nothing common about any of this.

"No,'' he said emphatically, then glanced up at her. Seeing her confused expression, he explained, "I want to give her time to see me in a different light. The only time we've been in each other's company is at the—'' Lord, he'd almost said "office.'' If he wasn't careful he'd blow this whole thing, and just when everything was going so well. "I mean at college and then later at some of her brother's business gatherings.''

"I take it her brother is in insurance?''

He nodded, then wondered if he should reach up and feel his nose to see if it was growing longer.

Bernadette took a bite of her hot dog. She chewed it slowly while thinking over all Nick had said. "Maybe you're right. Timing is important.''

"I just don't want to put her off by jumping the gun,'' he explained to her. "And at least this way I can enjoy her company before I open myself up for a flat-out rejection.''

There was a hint of resignation in his expression. It was almost like he was saying, "I know I'm going for the gold, and there's every possibility I'll lose out, but I'm going to make a valiant try, anyway.''

Bernadette reached over and touched his hand. "You must love her a great deal."

Nick's eyes lifted to hers while his thumb moved over her index finger, then softly slid down its length. "Yes, I do," he said.

Chapter Five

Bernadette had never been so aware of a man's touch, his look. She suddenly felt warm all over, and it was all she could do to pull her hand back to her side of the table.

"Doreen is a lucky woman," she murmured, her eyes dropping to her plate. It wouldn't do to look him in the face. He might see something in her eyes that would embarrass them both.

"I'm hoping she'll think so," he replied, then surprised her by adding, "Bernadette, if you don't mind, I'd rather not talk about Doreen tonight."

That was strange coming from a man who was supposedly in love with the woman. However, Bernadette was so relieved at the idea of not having to discuss Doreen that she didn't question him about it.

"I don't mind at all," she said, trying her best not to sound too pleased. She looked up at him then and decided the best thing to do would be to change the conversation completely.

"Is your hot dog okay?"

"Very good," Nick answered, greatly relieved that she'd agreed to drop the subject of Doreen without dispute. He didn't know how he could have handled it if she had. "It's been a long time since I've eaten one. Mother always considered hot dogs and hamburgers as junk food, so I never really acquired a taste for them."

Bernadette was thoroughly amazed. "She must have been terribly strict."

He shook his head as he swallowed a bite of food. "Not really. My parents were never the kind who said, 'Nicholas, you can't do this' or 'You must do that.' They always believed I was above that. They merely set certain standards and expected me to live up to them. Sometimes I think they believed I came from the nursery as an adult."

Bernadette reached for her soft drink while giving him a puzzled look. "Nick, that's rather harsh, isn't it?"

She watched him eat the French fries, inwardly pleased to see him eating with a big appetite.

"You have to know that my mother and father were told they could never have children. I came along when most couples are planning their retirement. I was a big interruption in their lives, and I guess I always sensed that as I was growing up. I suppose that's why I was never a rebellious child. I didn't want to make more of a nuisance of myself than I already was."

Bernadette couldn't imagine anything sadder than a child believing he was a nuisance to his parents.

"Nick," she countered huskily, "you could never have been a nuisance."

He gave her a rueful smile. "Maybe, maybe not. What about you, Berny? Were you ever a little rebel?"

She laughed. "Only when I didn't get my own way."

He chuckled. "That sounds very much like you," he said.

Their talk moved on to other things as they finished their meal. They discussed the report they were working on and the sale he was trying to negotiate. They were stuffed by the time Bernadette suggested they move to the living room.

Motioning for Nick to take a seat on the flowered couch, Bernadette sat down on the carpet beside the stereo. To one side of the hi-fi system there was a stack of LPs in a wooden crate. Nick leaned back, crossed his ankles and watched Bernadette's thoughtful expression as she flipped through the albums.

"Well," Bernadette said after a while, "the one record I'm looking for is the one I can't find."

"It doesn't matter," he hastened to assure her. "It would probably be better all around if we'd forget this whole thing about the dancing and the party."

Bernadette looked at him as if he just suggested committing murder. Rising to her feet, she hurried over to him.

"Oh, no, Nick. Please don't back out on me. I'm so looking forward to your being there."

He frowned, disbelieving. "I don't know why. As I told you, I'm not the dancing, whooping-it-up type."

Bernadette sank down on the edge of the couch next to him. "How do you know you're not that type? You might surprise yourself."

His frown changed to a wry look. "I haven't gotten much experience in the past few years. It's been a long time since I've done any partying."

"I thought you executives were always having parties?"

Again frowning, he shook his head. "Those aren't parties. They're just gatherings where everyone sips cocktails, talks business and tries not to look bored."

Bernadette laughed at his description. "Well, this party won't be like that at all," she told him firmly.

One of his dark brows arched with dry humor. "That's exactly why I don't belong there."

"Nick," she scolded gently, "it will be great fun. And it will give me a chance to show you off."

He turned an astounded look on her. "Show me off," he repeated. "Berny, I think we should take you to that optical place. You're definitely not seeing clearly."

She laughed softly and reached over to squeeze his forearm. "My vision hasn't changed, I can assure you. And I can't wait to see everyone's faces when they see you without your glasses."

He groaned and raked a hand through his hair. "Believe me, Berny. I'm not anticipating that moment."

"But why?"

"Why? Because I've just never been one to want to draw attention to myself. I'm a stay-in-the-background person. That's where I belong."

"That's the most ridiculous thing I've ever heard. I can't imagine where that came from and why you're so unsure of yourself around people."

She watched his eyelids lower behind his glasses, and she sensed that he wanted to hide from her now.

She was beginning to realize that maybe that was what he'd been doing all along with keeping himself in the background—hiding.

"I'm not unsure of myself when I'm faced with business matters," Nick said quietly. "I can deal with the most temperamental clients anyone could imagine. But when it comes to more personal things I turn into a bumbling idiot."

Bernadette shook her head. "No! Don't say that. You're not like that at all."

He sent her a sidelong glance. "I'll bet your friends at the office won't agree with you."

She felt herself blushing as she recalled some of the things Joyce and Nigel had said about Nick. "They— they think you're rather cold."

His eyes widened at this bit of news. Cold? God, he felt anything but cold sitting here beside Bernadette, her hand still on his arm. "Is that what you think of me?"

She cocked her head to one side, wondering if her opinion really mattered to him. She hoped it did. "No, but then I know you. I know that you're a warm, kind, considerate person. So why don't you want others to see that part of you? I'm certain now that you wear those drab suits and hairstyle because you want to avoid any kind of attention."

"Drab? I merely dress like the other executives," he reasoned.

"Yes, but the other executives are in their sixties," she countered. "When I first went to work for you I thought you were just attending a lot of funerals. Now I know it's just all a camouflage."

"Funerals? Camouflage?" He let out a heavy breath. "You're tough, Berny."

Her soft laugh dismissed his words. "No, I'm not tough. I just want you to know that you're not a man who belongs in the background and that I don't want you to stay there."

Nick leaned his head back and laughed with amazement. "Oh, Berny, I'm certainly not a man to be spotlighted."

Her face serious, she tightened her fingers on his arm and pressed on. "But why do you think that way, Nick?"

His face lost its humor. "Why are any of us the way we are, Berny? I don't know. Maybe it started when I was a child. I know there were times I craved to hear a word of praise from my parents. And I never did."

"What did you want to hear?"

From behind his glasses, Nick let his eyes glide over Bernadette's face. Her skin had a luminescent quality. At the moment, her cheeks were tinged with a delicate pink that made her blue eyes seem to sparkle even more. He tried to remember some of the women he'd encountered through the years, but it was impossible to conjure up even one image with Bernadette so close to him, so fresh and beautiful. Two years ago, when she'd walked into his office for the first time, the word 'woman' had taken on a new meaning for Nick. In that time the definition hadn't changed.

"Well, just once I'd liked to have heard 'Nick, you played a good game of soccer,'" he said finally.

"Were you good at soccer?"

"I wasn't shabby," he said without conceit. "I made the varsity team."

"Is that all you wanted to hear? Just that you played good soccer?" Bernadette went on.

His mouth twisted to a mocking curve. "It would have helped to have heard 'Nick's growing into a fine-looking young man,' or at least to have gotten my hair ruffled by my mother or my shoulder slapped by my father."

Bernadette's blue eyes softened. It was easy to see him as that young boy, wanting and needing a simple sign of affection from his parents but never getting it. These past two years she'd known him, he'd always projected such a stern, no-nonsense personality. She was beginning to understand why.

"But that never happened," she said gently, already knowing the answer.

He shook his head. "No, but I often heard 'Nick's going to make a million before he's thirty-five.' It was an expectation pinned on me at the age of thirteen."

Her brows arched very high. "Well, have you?"

His gaze met hers straight on. "No. But then I'm not thirty-five yet, and I need only a few dollars to get there."

Bernadette burst into uproarious laughter. She couldn't help herself. He was so deadpan about being a millionaire.

After a moment, Nick joined in her laughter. Bernadette had a way of making him see the lighter side of things, of making him feel good about himself in spite of everything.

"Hell, I'm only thirty," he said as if he was only just realizing it himself. "I may make two million by the time I'm thirty-five."

"You probably will," she agreed, laughter still running through her voice. "So why are you so unsure about yourself?"

His eyes met hers then dropped to her fingers still curled around his forearm. "I'm not—I—"

"Nick, will you take off your glasses?"

"What?"

Bernadette didn't repeat the question. Instead, she leaned closer and slowly pulled them from his face. He blinked once, then seemed to focus on her face.

"Why are you looking at me like this?" he asked, unaware that his voice had dropped to a husky murmur.

"Because," she said softly, "I'm trying to figure out why you don't see what I see when I look at you."

"Berny—" he began breathlessly.

"Are you shortsighted?"

"Yes. Why?"

She took him by the hand and pulled him up from the couch. "Because I want to show you something. Come here with me."

Nick allowed her to lead him across the floor while trying to figure what she was about. She stopped in front of a gold-edged mirror hanging on a wall.

"Can you see yourself this far?" she asked.

"Just a blurred image," he replied.

She moved him a few steps closer to the mirror. "How about now?"

He nodded. "It's pretty clear now," he told her then shot her a wary look. "Is this going to be painful?"

Bernadette giggled and took hold of his chin. "No. It should feel good," she assured him, then pointed his face so that his reflection and hers stared back at them. "All I want you to do is take a look at yourself."

"Bernadette," he protested, "I see myself in the mirror every morning when I shave."

"But obviously you don't really look at it or you would know you're a good-looking man."

"Berny, you're patronizing me and—"

She'd been looking at their images in the mirror, but now her face jerked angrily around to his. "I don't try to patronize or flatter anyone, Nicholas Atwood!"

Nicholas was so overwhelmed by her closeness that he almost forgot what they were saying. Her fingers were still on his face, her lips were only inches away. If he was such an intellectual, why couldn't he think rationally now?

"Berny, I—"

Her frustrations shattered at the confusion in his voice. "It's true, Nick, just trust me." Her fingers lifted from his chin and touched the corner of his eye. "Your eyes are a vivid blue. Just like the sky after it rains. Your brows and lashes are thick and dark, like your hair."

Nick swallowed as her fingers slid down his cheek. He hoped this examination wouldn't last much longer. He didn't know how much control he had left.

"You've got a strong, square, masculine jawline and—" her finger lightly trailed down "—a lot of men would kill for that dent in your chin."

"It's—it's a pain to—to shave around," he said, unaware that his voice had changed to a whisper.

Her fingers walked softly up his chin. Nick had to stifle a groan as her forefinger outlined his upper lip.

Bernadette's brown eyes focused drowsily on his lips. "Your mouth is nice, too, Nick. Especially when it's smiling. Nice for talking, nice for smiling, nice for kissing."

Her voice dropped lower with each word. Of its own will, her face leaned into his. She couldn't stop herself. She had to taste that mouth, had to feel his warmth against her.

Closing her lips over his, she was hardly aware of the husky growl in Nick's throat. She was too entranced by his sweet, masculine taste. In less than a second, her arms had moved around his neck and her fingers had slid through his hair and pressed against his scalp.

Nick was quick to follow. His arms went around her and pressed the small of her back, causing her to arch with pleasure against him.

The movement crushed her full breasts against his chest. Nick was so lost he had the feeling they were falling to the floor. When he realized they weren't, he decided that if she kept on kissing him this way that's where they needed to be.

Bernadette wriggled closer to him, moaning softly in her throat as his mouth made a passionate exploration of hers. In that moment, she knew she wanted to be the only one he kissed this way, that she wouldn't allow another woman to receive this same delight. Another woman! Doreen!

Her mind screeched to a shocking halt. She stiffened and jerked away from him so abruptly that Nick swayed on his feet.

"Oh, Nick! I—I—" Her hands flew to her face and she whirled away from him with mortal humiliation. "I'm so sorry! Doreen—I forgot all about her."

She was apologizing for that! His senses were still reeling, and he wanted nothing more than to pull her back in his arms and kiss her until she forgot she'd ever heard the name Doreen.

"You must think that I'm . . . promiscuous or—"

"Berny," he said, taking a step toward her, "don't say that. I think you're . . . very special."

Dropping her hands from her cheeks, she slowly turned back to him. "Do you really think so, Nick?"

Her voice was husky, and he wondered if she'd been as aroused as he had.

"Of course I think so."

She smiled tremulously and said, "I guess you think I was trying to seduce you."

God, he certainly hoped so! But that was the last thing he could tell her. "I—I've never been seduced by a beautiful woman before. It would be nice to think that you were the first."

Bernadette forced herself to laugh. It came out very shakily, but she knew she had to try and play this light. He wasn't serious about her. He was serious about Doreen. God, what was happening to her? What was this man doing to her?

"It's just that you're very endearing, Nick, and I, well—" She couldn't go on. She didn't know how to go on without making a bigger fool of herself. "Well, maybe we'd better forget all this and get on with the dancing."

Nick watched her cross the room and pick up the telephone. What was he going to do about all this? Damn it, he'd painted himself into a corner. If he tried to come out now, things were sure to get messy. No, he'd have to ride this thing out until the right time presented itself.

Bernadette punched some numbers, then said, "Hi, Lawrence. How's my sweetie?"

Nick stiffened in his tracks as Bernadette went on. "Listen, do you have my Mellencamp album?"

This Lawrence guy must have answered yes, Nick thought, because Berny went on to say, "Yes, that's the one. Can you bring it over? Right now? Great! Thanks, honey."

Nick jammed his fists down in his pants pockets and walked back to the couch. "Look, Berny, this is too much trouble, and maybe I'd—"

She quickly waved away his words. "It's no trouble, Nick. Lawrence doesn't mind. He'll be right over."

Just what he was afraid of, Nick thought, his spirits sinking. At this moment he didn't know if he could face another one of Bernadette's boyfriends. But he sat down on the couch, anyway.

Moments later, a knock sounded on the door. Berny called "Come in," and Nick cut his eyes toward the doorway to see a towheaded boy.

Lawrence crossed the threshold with a blast of cold air and sauntered importantly into the room. The album was cradled safely beneath one arm.

"Hi, Berny! Here's the album," he announced, then caught sight of Nick on the couch.

Bernadette hurried over to introduce them. "Nick, this is Lawrence. And Lawrence, this is Nick Atwood, my boss."

Lawrence walked over to where Nick was sitting. "How do you do, sir?" he asked, extending his hand to Nick in a grown-up manner.

Nick shook it with equal solemnity. "Hello, Lawrence."

Lawrence glanced back up at Berny who was standing beside him. "Is this the guy you work for at that insurance place?"

She nodded. "He's the one," she said proudly.

Lawrence's eyes widened back on Nick. "Gee! You're a pretty nice guy."

Nick smiled faintly, wondering about the sudden praise. "Really? Why do you say that?"

"'Cause you gave Berny that raise. She was gonna have to move 'cause she'd just bought her Z28, and she couldn't pay for it and her rent, too. But then you gave her more money and she didn't have to move," he explained.

"Lawrence!" Bernadette exclaimed.

Unaffected, the boy looked at her. "It's all right to tell your boss something like that, Berny. I wouldn't tell nobody else," he promised.

"You better not, Motor Mouth," she warned.

Nick smiled with amusement. "I take it that it made you happy because Bernadette didn't have to move?"

Lawrence nodded enthusiastically, and Nick added, "I'm glad about that. But I'm not actually the one who pays Bernadette. I just saw to it that she got the extra money."

"Berny says you're really smart. She says you can do all kinds of calculations in your head and that you know more about business than the people on Wall Street do."

Bernadette felt herself blushing. Nick glanced up to meet her gaze. In that moment he felt very close to her, and the urge to reach out and touch her was overwhelming. He forced himself to look back at young Lawrence.

"That was nice of Berny to say. But just between you and me, I think she's a bit biased," Nick told the boy.

"Biased? What's that?" he asked, looking at Bernadette and then back to Nick.

"That means since I'm her boss she might say things about me that are, well, a little exaggerated."

"Nick," Bernadette protested as Lawrence shook his head.

"Berny always says exactly what she means." He grinned beguilingly up at Bernadette. "You remember, Berny, when I wanted that street bike with all the chrome on it and you told me I didn't need it and that I just wanted it 'cause it was all shiny and flashy."

Bernadette nodded. "Oh, yes. I remember well."

"I got real mad at Berny," Lawrence told Nick. "I thought she was just saying all that stuff. But it turned out she was right and the bike tore up right after I got it."

Nick wanted to laugh, but somehow he managed to keep a straight face.

"Bernadette is a smart lady. You should listen to her," he advised Lawrence.

"Yeah, she is," Lawrence agreed, then gave Nick a guarded look. "Say, you're not gone on her, are you? 'Cause Berny's waiting for me to grow up and marry her."

Nick turned an amazed look on Bernadette. She lowered herself to the couch while giving Lawrence a conspiratorial wink.

"Lawrence is the only boyfriend I've ever had whom I wanted to keep indefinitely," she explained to Nick. "So what do you think? Is he good husband material?"

Nick made a show of looking Lawrence over from head to toe. "Well, he looks strong enough, and he's good-looking. What about security, Lawrence? Have you thought of how you're going to support Bernadette?"

"Support her?" he repeated, his small face wrinkled with confusion.

"Yes, you know—a job."

"You mean I'll have to have a job and make money?" Lawrence asked in an astounded voice.

"That's usually the way it works," Nick told him. "Bernadette might want a new Z28 after you get married."

"And I'd have to buy it for her?"

Bernadette and Nick laughed at Lawrence's panicked response. Nick said, "It would be the manly thing to do."

Lawrence looked over to Bernadette with a pleading expression. "Gee, Berny, do you think you could give me a little time to play football before we get married?"

Bernadette smiled indulgently at her little friend. "I'm sure we can work something out, Lawrence. So how about you going over to the stereo and putting that record on for me?"

Lawrence hopped to do her bidding. After a matter of moments the loud rock music reverberated throughout the room.

"Turn it down, Lawrence," Berny quickly told him.

"But Berny," the boy protested, "that's where the volume was."

"I know, but I want to be able to talk to Nick without yelling. I'm going to teach him a little dancing."

Lawrence turned down the volume then looked eagerly to Nick and Berny. "Can I stay and help?"

"Can you dance?" Nick spoke up.

Lawrence nodded readily. "Berny taught me. I thought it was sissified at first. But then she told me how football players use dancing sometimes in their training, like ballet.''

Bernadette pursed her lips at the child. ''That wasn't the only reason, Lawrence. It won't be long until you're going to junior high school. I don't want you standing against the wall during all those school dances.''

As he had, Nick thought. He hadn't thought it mattered then. His parents had insisted there were more important things to occupy his mind than dancing, girls and sports. Nick hadn't realized how much he'd missed until Bernadette had come into his life.

''Well, Lawrence, if Berny doesn't mind your staying, then I certainly don't,'' Nick spoke up.

Bernadette smiled at both of them, thinking it would probably be better for her if Lawrence did stay. Maybe his presence would keep her from making an idiot out of herself as she had earlier.

''That's fine with me. So come on, Nick. Get on your feet and show us what you can do.''

For the next thirty minutes, as rock music blared in the background, Nick found himself pushed, prodded and bent into all kinds of outrageous positions. Yet Bernadette and Lawrence made learning to dance seem like something to laugh about. And all three of them did it heartily. In fact, they were having such a fun time that they nearly missed the sound of the telephone ringing.

Lawrence hurried to answer it. ''Bernadette Baxter's residence,'' he spoke, then groaned. ''Aw Mom, do I have to? We're dancing, and Berny's—'' He listened for a few moments, then said, ''Okay,'' mumbling with disappointment.

After he placed the telephone back in its cradle Bernadette asked, "You have to go home?"

He nodded gloomily. "I haven't finished my math for tomorrow."

"Don't pout about it," Bernadette told him. "You can come back over another day."

"But Nick may not be here," he said.

"I'll invite him over," Bernadette promised.

"We'll get together again," Nick assured him. "I might even have that moonwalk down by the time I see you again."

Lawrence chuckled at that, and Bernadette said, "Now you better be going before your mother gets mad at both of us. Thank you for bringing the album over, Lawrence."

"You're welcome. Bye now," he said, then trotted out the door.

A gust of cold air rushed in as Lawrence shut the door behind him. Bernadette shivered and wrapped her arms around her.

"Now that Lawrence is gone, why don't we take a break and have some coffee?" she suggested.

"Sounds nice," Nick agreed.

Bernadette motioned toward the couch. "Go ahead and take a seat. I'll bring it in."

She went to the kitchen and quickly fetched two mugs of coffee along with a few cookies she'd baked earlier.

"Lawrence likes you. I can tell," she said with a smile as she returned to the living room. "I hope you didn't consider him a pest. Children get on some people's nerves."

He took the mug she offered him. "On the contrary, I enjoyed him very much. I've always wanted children of my own. And definitely not just one."

Bernadette joined him on the couch and carefully rested her coffee on her crossed legs. "Really? Me, too. I hated being an only child. Did you?"

He nodded. "Despised it. When I was very small I even made up an imaginary brother to play with. But that came to a stop when Mother threatened to send me to a child psychologist."

"Good Lord," Bernadette exclaimed. "She thought that was abnormal? I had two imaginary playmates. One was a sister and the other a friend. I wonder what your mother would have thought about me?"

Nick's chuckle was filled with humor. "I imagine Mother would have quite a bit to say about you."

Bernadette gave him a sidelong glance, her eyes crinkling with amusement at the corners. "Tell me. I'm curious."

His laughter deepened and he shook his head. "I don't really think you'd want to hear it, Berny."

"Why?" she asked a bit indignantly.

"Because she'd say you were an eighties woman."

"I *am* an eighties woman."

He smiled and sipped his coffee. "I know."

"I take it your mother doesn't like that type of woman?"

"You have to know that Mother comes from a prominent old family in Boston. She was raised with very rigid views. It's still with her."

"Sounds like my grandmother. She thought I would be labeled 'loose' when I moved into my own apartment," Bernadette told him with a laugh. "I still haven't quite figured how she got up enough nerve to use that word in front of me."

Nick's expression became guarded as he reached for a cookie from the silver tray. "Do you...have friends over here a lot?" he asked.

Bernadette's brows lifted as she tried to decipher what he meant by friends. "Sometimes. Why?"

His complexion suddenly darkened a shade. "You have lots of men friends. I just wondered if—"

"If I ask them over like I have you?" she finished for him.

He nodded, desperately wishing he could have kept his mouth shut. He couldn't imagine how she was viewing the personal question.

She shook her head. "No. I don't actually. I've had mixed groups here before, but never just one man. Until you."

"Forgive me, Berny. That was terribly crass of me to ask you such a thing," he said looking down into the coffee dregs in his mug.

Bernadette crunched blithely into a cookie. "Think nothing of it, Nick. I know that most people at Sooner Fidelity think of me as a Marilyn Monroe, sex-goddess type, and that I have men for breakfast, lunch and dinner. But it simply isn't so. True, I have lots of friends who happen to be men, but I consider my home something very private and personal. I'd have to feel very close to a man before I invited him into my home."

He looked at her. "You invited me."

The cookie she was about to bite into stopped before it reached her mouth. "Yes. But you're different."

He frowned. "You mean safe, don't you?"

Safe? He was anything but safe. Earlier, when they had kissed, Bernadette had wanted nothing more than for their embrace to go on and on.

"That isn't what I meant at all," she told him, a bit flustered. "You're not like other men. I trust you not to hurt me."

Hurt her? Was she afraid of being hurt by a man? It didn't seem possible. "I've enjoyed the dancing," he said, feeling the need to change the subject for her sake and his. "You're a good teacher."

She smiled at him. "I had a good student. So are you feeling better about the Christmas party now?"

He nodded. "I'll give it a try. For your sake."

She smiled to herself, glad that he hadn't said for Doreen's sake. Setting her empty cup on the table, she said, "We haven't done any slow dancing. Want to try a little of that?"

Nick knew he should scream a big, loud no. Instead, he heard himself saying, "Whatever you think."

Rising from the couch, Bernadette went over to the stereo. She took a long time choosing the album to play. When the music did start, it was mostly slow drums and alto sax. It was very soulful-sounding, but more than that, it was sexy. Nick downed the dregs in his mug, trying to push lustful thoughts out of his mind.

"Ready?" she asked, coming to stand before him.

"Ready? Sure." He put down the mug and rose to his feet.

Bernadette took his hand and he put his free arm around her shoulders. He began to move her to the music.

"You're holding me too far away from you. You could drive a freight train between us."

He gently pulled her up closer and wondered if his lungs would remember to breathe in and out without his telling them to. "Is this better?"

"Much," she answered, realizing how perfectly their bodies fit together. She liked the feel of him against her. Liked it all too much.

"Then I'm passing the test?"

"You're very light on your feet, Nick, but the muscles in your neck are as stiff as a board."

"I'm stiff?" he asked, then suddenly looked down at her and chuckled. "That was a stupid question, wasn't it? I'll bet you've always thought I was stiff."

Their faces were mere inches apart. She looked into his and found she loved the laughter and teasing she found there. "Actually I've always been a bit awed by you," she confessed with a broad smile.

His dark brows knitted together. "Awed? You make me sound like some feudal lord who had to be tiptoed around."

"Well," she said, "your brilliance is a bit awesome. At first I was afraid I might fall short in your eyes."

"That's absurd. You're just as brilliant. It's just directed into other channels."

She laughed softly and squeezed his hand. "We make a wonderful pair, both being so brilliant and all."

He smiled back at her. "We are rather dazzling," he agreed.

Bernadette sighed and rested her head against his shoulder. It was so pleasant to be with him like this, so satisfying to feel his warmth next to her. She lifted her face to his. "We'd make lovely children together."

The astounded look in his eyes had Bernadette quickly adding, "Relatively speaking, that is."

He took a deep breath and released it slowly. "Relatively speaking," he repeated, "they would be lovely."

Her blue eyes were full of warmth and something else Nick couldn't quite describe. Could it be caring? Was it possible that this bright, beautiful woman could actually care for him?

Bernadette rested her cheek against his and gave herself up to the music and the pleasure of his touch.

Nick lifted his hand from her shoulder and touched her hair. It was like sliding his fingers through golden silk. She was a golden girl through and through, he thought, with her dazzling smile, the warm light in her eyes and her kind, generous heart.

If Nick had any sense at all he'd step away from her, end the dance and be on his way home. But home was that cold monstrosity of a house with no one in it. He didn't want to leave Bernadette to face its emptiness. He didn't want to leave Bernadette, plain and simple.

Phase two had, in many ways, worked out far better than he'd hoped. But it had also created problems that Nick had failed to foresee. He wasn't going to dwell on them tonight. It was still at least a week and a half until the New Year. He intended to make the most of it.

Chapter Six

"Berny, I want to know what's going on," Joyce said, grabbing Bernadette by the arm and jerking her into one corner of the coffee lounge.

"What do you mean?" Bernadette asked with feigned innocence.

Joyce shot her a mocking glare. "You know perfectly well. Practically everyone saw you and Mr. Atwood today at lunchtime obviously returning to the building—together," she explained coyly.

Bernadette smiled coolly at her friend. "Yes, what about it?"

"What about it? This is the second time you were out with him!"

Bernadette glanced around the room. It was two thirty, and several other people were grouped inside the small room to enjoy the fifteen-minute coffee break. "Can you keep your voice down, Joyce? And actually you're wrong, it was more than the second time."

"And he wasn't wearing his glasses!" Joyce hissed. Then staring at Bernadette with an incredulous look, she said, "You've been out with him more than twice?"

Bernadette frowned. "Nigel must be losing it," she muttered, fully expecting that he'd already told Joyce about the cufflinks Nick had left on her dashboard.

"Old lady Whitfield has been keeping Nigel very busy. Why? What does he know that I don't?"

"Didn't you think Nick looked great?" Bernadette asked, ignoring Joyce's last question.

"Looked great?" Joyce repeated, then placed a worried hand on Bernadette's brow. "My dear, come here and let me help you sit down. Obviously you're coming down with something."

Bernadette glared at Joyce, who tugged her over to the vinyl couch and pushed her down on one end.

"Joyce, don't be sarcastic with me. I'm very serious about this. Now, didn't you think Nick looked great?"

Joyce joined her on the couch. "Has he been feeding you something, dropping something in your coffee?"

"Why?"

"It's apparent to me that he's put you into some kind of hypnotic daze. It *has* to be some kind of drug. Maybe it's something you're inhaling, like his cologne?"

"Nick's cologne is very nice," Bernadette retorted.

"That's it then!"

"Joyce," Bernadette warned and started to get up.

Joyce clamped a hand over her friend's shoulder. "Okay, okay," she relented. "To tell you the truth, I was so stunned at seeing the two of you together again that I didn't really notice how he looked without the glasses."

Bernadette relaxed and smiled eagerly at Joyce. "He has the sexiest blue eyes, Joyce. Who would have believed it?"

"Sexy? Definitely not I."

Bernadette frowned and sipped the coffee from the Styrofoam cup she held in her hand. "I know nearly everyone has misconceptions about Nick. But that's just because they don't know him."

Joyce was looking more stunned by the moment. "Who would want to? He's a stuffed shirt who looks down on other employees as mere peons."

"You're way off base, Joyce. Nick is nothing like that. He's kind, considerate, very humble and fun."

"You are talking about Nicholas Atwood, executive vice president of sales, the man who has been your boss for the past two years?"

Bernadette nodded. "I am."

"It's like I said at first, you've either been drugged or—" Joyce's eyes opened wide. "You're not falling for this guy, are you? No, I won't even ask you that question. It's unthinkable. You and Atwood—it would be like pairing up fire and ice."

Bernadette smiled pointedly. "Put them together and the ice melts every time."

"Berny, really!"

Ignoring Joyce's dismay, she rose to her feet and dropped the cup into the trash. "Like I said, you're way off base, Joyce." She started out the door, only to have Joyce jumping to her feet to follow.

"Berny, I can see this is serious! You're worrying me. You know it? I've never seen you acting so...so serious!"

"Thanks, Joyce. I didn't know I was always such a big joke."

"Why are you wearing that black jersey today?"

Bernadette looked down at her dress. It had a dropped waist and three-quarter-length sleeves. The dress draped her body gently but still seductively. "I often wear this dress to work."

"And you've got your hair up! And I can tell those are real pearls you're wearing in your ears! I suppose you're going to tell me you wear them all the time, too?"

"Don't you know anything about pearls? The more you wear them the better they look. The natural oil from your skin keeps them—"

"You're evading the point."

Bernadette took a deep breath. "That's because there is no point. Nick and I have become friends. He's left his glasses behind for a pair of contacts. Nothing earth-shattering has happened, I assure you."

Joyce folded her arms across her breast. "Then can you tell me, unequivocally, that you haven't fallen for the man?"

"Unequivocally? Am I on trial here, or have you been hanging around Nigel for too long?" she asked with dry humor.

"Berny—"

"I can't fall for Nick. He has—" Bernadette clamped her mouth shut, turned on her heel and walked away. She'd almost said he already had his sights on another woman. She couldn't let Joyce know that. She didn't even want to know it herself.

"Berny, come back here," Joyce called after her in a loud whisper.

Bernadette glanced back over her shoulder at her friend. "We're late. Get back to work," she hissed.

Later, on her drive home from work, Bernadette thought a lot about Joyce's question. Was she honestly falling for Nick? She was afraid her friend might be right.

Bernadette had been dazzled by some of the men she'd known. But that's all it had been—just infatuation. She could not remember thinking of any man the way she did of Nick. He reminded her of the deeper, more serious side to her. He reminded her that some day she would grow tired of the single life, that some day she would want someone to share her life, give her children.

Perhaps under other circumstances that would be good. Those things would give her life a fullness, a meaning it was now lacking. But as it was, she was being a fool to think of Nick in a romantic way. Doreen stood between them like an invisible wall.

With sudden decision, Bernadette steered the Z28 onto the next off-ramp. She hadn't seen her mother in a few days. For some inexplicable reason she needed to see her now.

A few minutes later, Bernadette let herself into her mother's house and called out to her.

"In here, darling," a voice answered.

Bernadette followed the voice and found her tall, brown-haired mother in the bathroom, winding her hair up in hot rollers. Bernadette kissed her mother's cheek.

"So what's up, love?" the older woman asked.

Bernadette shrugged. "I was on my way home and thought I should check on you."

"Check on me? How sweet you are."

Barbara Baxter was a beautiful woman. She'd given birth to Bernadette at a very young age and was just now reaching her early forties. Or maybe it was more like blossoming into instead of reaching. She didn't look a day past thirty-five. Bernadette was very proud of her mother. She also loved her deeply and could usually talk to her about anything. Funny, now that she was here, she was reluctant to bring up the subject of Nick.

"Going somewhere?"

Her mother nodded. "Staff party. The doctor is throwing it at his house in Nichols Hills. What should I wear?"

"Something red. You look beautiful in red." Bernadette sighed then leaned against the doorjamb.

"Is anything wrong, Berny? You seem sort of downcast. Hard day at work?"

"We're trying to finish the year-end report. It's been very busy." She watched her mother smooth beige foundation over her already perfect complexion. Each time she was with her mother she never failed to wonder what her father had seen in other women. How could he have cheated on someone as kind and beautiful as her mother? It never failed to leave a bitter, wasted feeling inside Bernadette whenever she thought of it.

"You say the party is at Nichols Hills? That's where Nick lives," Bernadette commented.

"Nick?"

"My boss. Mr. Atwood."

"Oh. So he's one of the affluent, too?"

Bernadette smiled wryly. "He should be. Sooner pays him a chunk of money."

"So we both have rich bosses. Maybe we should both make a play for them and wind up in Nichols Hills," Barbara suggested playfully.

Bernadette's smile was only halfhearted. "The dentist you work for is single?"

Her mother nodded. "Divorced. Rather nice-looking, too. Blond and muscular, witty."

Bernadette pulled a disgusted face. "I don't know how you could even think of marrying another man after the way Daddy treated you."

"Darling! You're talking nonsense. Your father is only one man in this world. They're not all like him," Barbara said.

"And how do you know that? Give them a questionnaire about cheating and hope they're not lying when they check off the answers?" she asked dryly.

"Berny, I don't like to hear you talking this way. If I can accept your father's shortcomings, then surely you can."

Bernadette momentarily closed her eyes. "He hurt you, Mother. He hurt me. I don't think I'll ever be able to completely forgive or forget."

Barbara set aside the bottle of foundation and turned toward her daughter. "You simply must, Berny. You'll never be happy if you don't. You'll never be able to have a lasting relationship with a man."

Bernadette pushed away from the doorjamb. "I don't want a lasting relationship. Dates are lasting enough for me."

Her mother shook her head sadly. "Darling, one of these days you're going to quit all this hopping around. You'll run into a man you'll want to have a lasting relationship with. Then it's going to be terribly hard on you—and him, too—if you're not able to trust."

Bernadette studied her mother thoughtfully. "You've never married again," she accused. "Obviously you haven't gotten over it."

Barbara began to dust blush across her high cheekbones. "I've never remarried because I haven't found a man I really love."

"Do you still love Daddy?"

She arched a brow at Bernadette. "In a way. I suppose a part of me will always love him. We lived many years together. We had you together. That kind of closeness doesn't just suddenly go away. But that doesn't mean I couldn't love another man," she added.

"Wouldn't you be afraid he'd do the same thing to you?"

Barbara applied lipstick. "No, I wouldn't." She lowered the lipstick and looked over to Bernadette. "Look, darling, it's very wrong of you to place all the guilt on your father. There's always two in a marriage. After we divorced I looked back and saw the many mistakes I made, like not giving him enough support and attention when he needed it."

Bernadette's gaze dropped to the floor. "There were lots of times I needed his support but he was away," she mumbled.

Her mother smiled with gentle understanding. "That's true, too. But you have to remember that he was only human, just a man. Even though he was your father. Mothers and fathers have a strike against them before they ever start out because they're expected to be perfect. No one can live up to that.''

Bernadette looked back up at her mother with a wary expression. ''Then I don't think I ever want to be a mother.''

Barbara countered that statement with a deep laugh. ''Oh, yes, honey. When you find the right man everything will just fall into place. You'll see. So what's all this serious talk about, anyway? Did your man stand you up tonight?''

Bernadette shook her head. ''No. I don't have a date for tonight,'' she said, then realized with dismay that she was disappointed because Nick hadn't wanted to get together tonight as they had the past two nights.

Her mother skirted around Bernadette and walked down the hall toward her bedroom. ''I'm glad you came by, honey,'' she told her daughter. ''I wanted to check with you about your plans for Christmas.''

Bernadette followed her mother. ''I hadn't really thought about Christmas Day, but I do know that I'll be attending a party Christmas Eve. Sooner is throwing a dance for its employees,'' she explained.

''Well, I hope you won't be disappointed, but I've been invited to go skiing at Taos over the Christmas holidays.''

''Mmm, that sounds nice,'' Bernadette said.

''Then you wouldn't be too put out with me if I wasn't here this time?''

Bernadette had always spent Christmas with her mother, but she hardly wanted to ruin her mother's opportunity to have a fun trip of skiing. Besides, she could always cook for herself. No doubt Lawrence would show up sometime during the day to show her all his gifts. And maybe Nick would like to come too, she thought. Her heart suddenly lifted as she smiled brightly at her mother. "Of course I wouldn't mind. You'll have a great time. And it will give me a chance to cook. I think I'll invite Nick."

"Your boss?" Barbara asked, turning her back to Berny so that she could do the zipper.

"Yes. His folks live on the West Coast so he'll probably be all alone."

"That's very thoughtful of you, honey. No one should be alone on the holidays."

Bernadette fastened the zipper, then smoothed the red dress across her mother's shoulders. "There. You look beautiful. And now I've got to go and let you finish getting ready."

"I'll call you before we leave for New Mexico," her mother said.

"I'll be mad if you don't," Bernadette said as she went through the door. "And if that dentist is as good as you say he is," she added mischievously, "then maybe you should go after him."

Her mother's reply was a trill of laughter.

Across town, Nicholas stood in front of his closet wearing nothing but a pair of jockey shorts and a disgusted frown.

Drab. Funerals. Sixty-five. Had Bernadette really seen his clothes that way? Damn it, he was a businessman. He was supposed to look professional, staid and no-nonsense.

He could just hear Bernadette's reaction to that. "But you can do it with a bit of flair and fashion, Nick."

The imagined comment brought a smile to his lips, and with a sudden impulse he pulled all the expensive, tailored suits off the hangers and tossed them onto the king-size bed. Hell, he thought. He was only thirty years old. It was about time he enjoyed being young. If anyone was smart enough or rich enough to get away with it, he was.

As the stack of clothes grew higher and higher, Nick felt better and better. And he almost laughed out loud when he imagined what his father would say if he knew Nick's intentions.

Once the closet was cleared, he hurriedly stepped into the khaki trousers he'd worn over to Bernadette's and put on an oxford-cloth shirt. Downstairs, he told the housekeeper to go home since he would be out and wouldn't require an evening meal. Then he asked her to call the Salvation Army to come collect the suits he'd piled on the bed.

He was whistling as he went downstairs.

The next morning, Bernadette was already working at her desk when Nick came through the door.

She looked up quickly from the typewriter to see him standing over her. It was Nick, but a different Nick. Slowly she pulled the glasses from her face and allowed her eyes to travel up and down his tall frame.

"Nick! What have you done?"

A sly gleam sparkled in the eyes that she could now see so well. "I went shopping. What do you think?"

"I think—" she got up from her chair and slowly circled him "—you look fabulous!"

His trousers were pleated with a distinctly Italian flavor. His jacket was unbuttoned, the material a slightly paler shade of brown than the slacks. Everything from his shoes to his shirt and tie reflected youth and were fashionable, but not overly so. He looked just right, and Bernadette, filled with glee, suddenly giggled.

"I knew you had great taste all along. What did you do with all the old suits?"

"Gave them to the Salvation Army," he answered with a solemnity that had Bernadette bursting into a fit of laughter.

He joined her with equal enthusiasm, and they both marveled and laughed even more at the idea of his tossing away thousands of dollars in clothes.

"And you've cut your hair," Bernadette exclaimed after their laughter had faded some. It had been clipped close to his head and flipped over to one side. "It's very preppie and cute and smart-looking."

"All those things?" he asked jokingly.

She smiled at him, her brown eyes lustrous. "I'm very proud of you, Nick."

He stepped toward her and unexpectedly took hold of her hand. "I didn't want to let you down at the Christmas Eve party."

Still smiling, she shook her head. "You wouldn't have let me down even if you hadn't changed a thing. When I say I'm proud of you, it's because you've decided to let the real you show through."

An incredible feeling swelled inside Nick's chest, and he had the strongest urge to pull her into his arms and kiss her until she was soft and limp and...ah, Berny, he silently sighed.

"Well, I'm definitely ready for the dance. Let's see if I still remember that step you taught me," he said, tugging her into his arms.

Laughing, Bernadette put her hand on his shoulder and began to match her movements to his. She wasn't going to remind him that it was early in the morning and that he hadn't even looked at the correspondence yet. He'd given Sooner Fidelity many long hours of overtime, and they were both enjoying the moment too much to spoil it.

A deep, male voice suddenly interrupted their fun. Both she and Nick turned surprised faces toward the door. It was Mr. Reynolds, president of sales. His office adjoined hers and Nick's. Apparently their laughter had disturbed him.

"Atwood? Is something wrong in here?"

Nick cleared his throat and reluctantly put Bernadette away from him. "No, sir. We were, er, just anticipating the Christmas party. Sorry if we disturbed you."

"Hell, boy, don't apologize," the gray-haired man exclaimed gruffly. "You've made this company. It's about time you relaxed a little."

With that, the older man winked at Bernadette and closed the door. Nick and Bernadette exchanged surprised glances, then burst into another gale of laughter.

The remainder of the week passed very quickly for Bernadette. She and Nick worked hard to finish the report, and somehow they managed to get it all done before the deadline.

Bernadette and Nick spent two nights Christmas shopping. The malls and shops were filled with throngs of shoppers, holiday music and special gift items.

Nick admitted that he'd never seen anyone shop as exuberantly as Bernadette did, and laughing, she had told him that she'd never seen anyone spend as much money as he did. He had waved away her words, saying it was nothing.

But it had seemed like a lot to Bernadette, particularly all the things he'd bought for Doreen. Bernadette had tried her best to forget about the unknown woman, but the gifts had brought Doreen to the forefront of things again. She'd had to admit to herself that she was jealous, and it had been extremely difficult to help Nick choose perfume, sexy nightwear and an outrageous pair of earrings for another woman.

Emeralds! Bernadette had bit down on her tongue in order to keep from telling him that Doreen couldn't possibly be worth emerald earrings, but he'd seemed so set on getting them that she'd merely nodded and smiled.

Bernadette shook the thoughts away. She wasn't going to be worrying about Doreen tonight. Tonight was the Christmas party, and Nick would be picking her up in less than an hour. She wanted to look dazzling for him. She wanted him to take one glance at her and forget all about that woman back in New York.

Perhaps that was playing dirty, but Bernadette didn't think so. From all Nick had told her, Doreen hadn't given him the time of day back when they'd gone to college together. If the woman had been too blind to see what a treasure he was, then Bernadette intended to take advantage of it.

She loved him. Yes, she loved him! It had scared her to admit it to herself. But seeing him buying all those things for Doreen had forced her to examine her feelings.

Her mother had said that someday Bernadette would find the right man. Well, Nick was that man even though he did have his heart set on someone else. She'd just have to turn it around some way. Show him that his secretary was really the right woman for him.

The weather had been growing colder and colder throughout the day. Bernadette knew she should probably wear slacks as the party was going to be casual. Yet she didn't want to be *that* casual. Bernadette had had a dress picked out for a week, and she wasn't going to let a little cold wind and snowflakes change her mind.

The knit dress was winter white, with a hint of angora that made it incredibly soft to the touch. She cinched in the waist with a wide red belt and matched it with red heels. After she'd curled her blonde hair rather tightly, Bernadette wound a wide piece of red lace through it and tied it in a bow.

Nick arrived to collect her five minutes early. Bernadette was glad. She had paced back and forth from the living-room picture window to the wall mirror in her bedroom. When she hadn't been watching for Nick, she'd been critically studying her appearance and wondering if she should change into something else.

It amazed her to realize she was so nervous. No man had ever made her feel nervous before, but she'd never wanted to please one like she did Nick.

There were snowflakes on his hair and the shoulders of his overcoat when she opened the door to let him in.

"My goodness! Is the weather getting that bad?" she asked.

"It looks like we're headed for a blizzard or ice storm," he said, his eyes warming with appreciation at the sight of her.

She looked festive and incredibly beautiful. "You look lovely, Berny. All the other women are going to pale beside you."

Bernadette smiled at him and drew in a shaky breath. A month ago she wouldn't have dreamed of Nicholas Atwood saying such a thing to her. She wouldn't have dreamed she would want to hear it so much.

"Thank you, Nick. Would you like coffee or something else before we start off?"

"I think we should get going before the streets get slick. But before we go—" He reached inside his coat pocket and pulled out a tiny white box tied with a red ribbon.

Bernadette looked at him with surprise when he held it out to her.

"I wanted to give you a little something to wear to the party tonight."

"Nick," she protested even as she took the box from his hands. "You didn't have to do this. Especially since I'm the one who forced you into going to this thing with me."

"You didn't force anyone into anything," he said gently, then his voice softened even more, "I hope you like it."

Bernadette lifted the lid to find a little gold reindeer with a diamond-studded collar around his neck. It was exquisite, and she knew just by looking that it was astonishingly expensive, something that would have taken her months to pay for. She couldn't believe it!

"Nick, I—I don't know what to say!"

He moved closer. "Why don't you just tell me whether you like it or not?"

"Like it?" She lifted her eyes from the reindeer up to his face. "It's beautiful, Nick, but I...feel very unworthy of this."

"Unworthy? What a silly thing to say," he countered.

"It's obviously very expensive, and you shouldn't be buying me such things."

He stepped even closer. "Why?"

"Why? Well—" she moistened her lips and met his vivid blue gaze "—because Doreen may find out. This would definitely be a strike against you."

He smiled at her, and Bernadette's breath caught in her throat. The expression on his face was nothing but sexy. Where had this come from? Had he been looking at her like this all along and she just hadn't noticed?

"Trust me, Berny. Doreen will never know about it."

"But—"

"Here," he said and took the box from her fingers. "Let me pin it on you."

Bernadette forced herself to stand motionless while he pinned the jewel over her left breast. She studied the top of his bent head and the dark waves of his hair, and noted the way his closeness made her knees quiver weakly. She wanted more than anything to lean forward and slide her arms around his neck. She wanted to place her lips on his and kiss him until they were both so breathless and crazy that neither one would care if they ever got to the party.

But how could Bernadette do that without looking like a wanton strumpet? Oh, dámn Doreen, or whoever you are, she thought.

As Nick pinned the reindeer to her dress, he struggled to keep his hands on the business of the moment. The thrust of her breast kept getting in the way of his arms and his thoughts. She smelled of sweet, sultry jasmine, and her breath was warm and seductive against the side of his neck. Instead of seeing the clip that fastened the pin, he saw himself folding her in his arms and kissing her until her brown eyes were limpid, then tearing her dress off and making long, languorous love to her.

But how could he do that, he wondered, without looking like a shallow liar and cheat? Oh damn, damn Nick! Why did you dream up Doreen in the first place? Because you love Bernadette, you idiot!

"There," he said huskily. "It may not be straight. But perhaps no one will notice."

Bernadette sucked in a jerky breath and looked down at the deer. "I can't imagine anything more beautiful, Nick. Do you think I could get by with wearing a reindeer all year long?"

He laughed softly, and the sound made her look up at his face. It was impossible to keep from stepping into his arms. She had to kiss him. She just had to. Doreen be hanged!

Nick's eyes drifted shut as her lips touched his, softly, gently. He had to stifle a groan when she finally stepped away from him.

"Thank you, Nick. This is the most marvelous gift I've ever had."

"You're very welcome, Bernadette," he said, returning her smile.

"Oh, my goodness," she said all of a sudden. "I've gotten red lipstick all over your mouth. Here, let me get it off before we leave. There's no telling what they'd be saying about us if you walked in wearing my lipstick!''

Laughing, she reached up and wiped the marks away with her forefinger. Nick clasped her hand in his before it fell away from his face. His expression grew serious as he looked down at her. "I really wouldn't care what they thought. Would you, Berny?"

Her blue eyes twinkled with newfound hope, and she smiled impishly back at him. Maybe he didn't care about this Doreen quite as much as he'd first believed, she thought. "Not a bit," she answered truthfully.

At first her answer appeared to please him. But then he suddenly cleared his throat and reached for her fur coat lying across the couch.

"I think we'd better be going," he said, quickly helping her into her coat.

They went out the door and stepped into the snowfall. As they walked down the drive to his car, Bernadette hugged Nick's arm to her side and looked up at the whitened sky. "This has got to be the most beautiful Christmas I can ever remember," she said.

Bernadette had made it that way for him, he thought. Whatever happened, she'd changed his life. He wasn't going to look back now. He hoped he'd never have to look back.

Chapter Seven

The wind was howling, carrying with it a stinging blanket of sleet, when Nick and Bernadette arrived outside the Sooner office building. Nick parked the car in an underground parking lot, and the two of them hurried to the elevator.

"I hope the nasty weather doesn't keep people home tonight," Bernadette said as the elevator swished upward for several floors. "It would be a shame after all the trouble and expense for the party."

"I noticed there were several cars in the parking area," Nick said. "At this time of year most people celebrate the holidays in spite of the weather."

They heard music as they stepped out of the elevator. Walking down a wide corridor, Bernadette reached for Nick's hand and was rewarded when he clasped his fingers around it and gave it a warm squeeze.

"I'm glad you're taking me to this dance, Nick," she confessed before they entered the room of merry-makers.

Nick looked down at her and smiled. "I'm glad I am too, Berny," he said.

There was warmth in his eyes and his voice. Bernadette tried not to think that one week from tonight he would be taking Doreen to the executive New Year's Eve party. That it was the time he'd chosen to tell Doreen he cared for her. Would he look at her with this same warmth?

No, don't think about it, Bernadette firmly told herself. Doreen wasn't here—yet. And tonight she fully intended to enjoy being with Nick and forget about the other woman.

Nick pushed open the wide double doors with one hand, keeping the other resting on the small of Bernadette's back, and he guided her into the room.

Bernadette was certain every eye in the room turned to look at the two of them. She didn't know if they were stunned by Nick's changed appearance or shocked by the two of them being together. Either way, they were receiving quite a few speculative stares.

The huge room had been decorated with shiny tinsel, holly and evergreen. In one corner was an enormous fir tree decorated with all sorts of beautiful Christmas ornaments. A few couples were already dancing. Others were clustered in small groups talking and enjoying the food and drinks, which were laid out on long buffet tables.

"Why don't we see what there is to eat?" Bernadette suggested. "I'm too hungry to dance just yet."

Nick smiled faintly. "I don't know if I can dance on a full stomach," he mused aloud.

Bernadette smiled encouragingly. "You'll be great. Just remember how we did it the other night."

That was just the problem, Nick thought. All he could remember about the other night was the way they'd kissed so passionately. If he held Bernadette in his arms tonight, how was he going to keep his mind on dancing? "I hope you're right," he murmured, guiding her across the room to where the food was located.

Bernadette piled her paper plate to dangerous heights with finger sandwiches, potato chips, dip and Christmas cookies, while urging Nick to do the same.

Several people spoke to them. Everyone knew who Nick was since his name was synonymous with Sooner Fidelity. They all knew Bernadette because she was friendly and made a point to know everyone who worked around her.

Once their plates were filled they sat down on folding chairs. Bernadette glanced around her as she munched on a chip slathered with creamy dip. She knew this room well since it usually housed the typing pool. Tonight there was no sign of a desk or typewriter.

"The room looks very festive," Bernadette spoke brightly. "Is this where the executive party will take place?"

Nick shook his head. "No, it will be in the board room down on the third floor."

"That stuffy room? How can you dance? There's carpet on the floor."

Nick's smile was wry. "I don't imagine there will be much dancing taking place."

Bernadette wondered what Doreen would think about that, then reminded herself to forget about the woman.

"Hi, Berny. Mr. Atwood."

The two looked up to see Joyce. She was dressed in a green jumpsuit and specks of ice glistened in her dark hair.

"Oh, hello, Joyce. Did you just come in?"

Joyce nodded while obviously noting how close Nick and Bernadette were sitting together. "The weather out there is atrocious! My car slid the last three blocks."

"Oh dear," Bernadette groaned, looking toward the row of glass windowpanes forming one wall of the room. They were wet, but that was about all she could see.

"Sounds like we're in for a winter storm," Nick commented.

"Well, as long as I made it here I'm going to forget about the weather and enjoy myself."

Bernadette noticed how Joyce's eyes kept sliding back to Nick. She knew the woman was taking in the difference in his appearance. Nick was wearing a shirt of deep burgundy and charcoal-gray stripes. His stylish slacks were the same gray. The dark color of his shirt made the vibrant blue of his eyes stand out that much more. He looked very handsome, and Joyce was definitely taking note of the fact.

Finally Joyce turned her attention to her. Her smile was feline as she said, "You're looking extra lovely, Berny. Did you risk driving your car tonight?"

Bernadette smiled with deliberate coyness for her old friend. She knew exactly what Joyce wanted to know. "Actually, no. Nick and I came together."

"Well," she said with an I-knew-you-were-getting-serious look, "I think I'll find myself something to eat. Excuse me."

"Of course," Nick said while Bernadette smiled faintly at her friend.

"Have you known Joyce for a long time?" Nick asked once the woman had moved away.

Bernadette nodded. "We started out in the typing pool here at Sooner. She still hasn't forgiven me for becoming your private secretary."

Nick frowned. "Why is that?"

Bernadette laughed lightly. "Because she's always believed you picked me for my legs."

Nick's first response was a surprised laugh, then he looked at Bernadette's legs with great interest. "I'm sorry to say I hadn't had the opportunity to see your legs before then. In fact, I had no idea what you looked like until you walked into my office that very first day."

Bernadette was surprised. "You really didn't know what I looked like?"

He shook his head as he bit into a sandwich. "I picked you because you had the best skills of anyone on the list. To be honest, I was expecting you to be sixtyish and gray-haired."

"I hope you weren't disappointed," she said with a questioning smile.

Disappointed! He'd been overwhelmed. "Your work has been far above what I expected in a secretary, Berny."

Bernadette's smile deepened. "I've always been proud of my legs, Nick, but I'm even prouder of my brain. You couldn't have given me a nicer compliment."

Bernadette was such a contradiction, he thought. She took her glamorous looks lightly, while on the other hand it would upset her terribly to think she'd made a mistake in her job.

The two took their time eating. It wasn't long before Joyce joined them, and then Nigel made an appearance with his fiery hair and flippant tongue.

Bernadette wondered how Nick would react to the wolf of data processing. It only took a few moments for her to see that Nick was quietly amused with Nigel. Bernadette was glad. She wanted Nick to like her friends, and in turn she wanted her friends to see the warm man that Nick really was.

By the time an hour had passed their group had multiplied. Several people from advertising and a few from accounting had joined them. The ones Nick knew he greeted warmly, the ones he didn't know Bernadette quickly introduced to him.

It was a long time before she and Nick had a chance to get on the dance floor, and when they finally did, Bernadette stepped eagerly into his arms.

"You're making a lot of friends tonight, Nick. They regard you highly for coming to a non-executive party when most of the other executives didn't bother themselves."

Nick's hand moved gently against her back. The sweater dress she was wearing was very soft, but not nearly as soft as her skin. His eyes were drawn to the dewiness of her parted lips. "Just because I hold a higher position doesn't mean I'm better than anyone here at Sooner. I'm sorry they've thought of me as a snob."

Berny shook her head. "They know better now. And the women are looking at you like you're fair game," she added, hoping the jealousy she was feeling wasn't showing. She'd never been possessive of any of her dates, but then she'd never cared for any of them as she did Nick. She loved him and she wanted to be able to let other women know that he belonged to her. But she didn't have that right and probably never would. Not if Doreen showed up next week.

Nick didn't care how many women looked at him. For him there was only one woman and he was holding her in his arms. He wished he could tell her that.

"I'm glad we're finally alone," he heard her saying. "There's something I wanted to ask you."

"What is it?"

She lifted her head from his shoulder to see that he was looking down at her with curiosity. "Tomorrow's Christmas Day," she said, "and my mother is going to be out of town."

"You must be disappointed."

Bernadette smiled up at him. "Actually I'm not. I wanted Mother to go and enjoy herself. But I will be disappointed if you don't agree to have dinner with me. I've already bought a turkey and all the trimmings. Will you come?"

She wanted to share Christmas dinner with him? It was more than he'd possibly hoped for. "I'm sure there are—that you'll have other guests to keep you company," he said quickly.

Bernadette shook her head. "No other guest," she assured him. "I want it to be just you and me—to celebrate our newfound friendship," she quickly added. "And since you'll be spending next weekend with Doreen, I figured this would be our last opportunity."

Nick wanted to groan with frustration at the mention of Doreen. He was beginning to wonder if it would be wise to wait until the New Year's Eve party to tell Bernadette his true feelings. But on the other hand, he didn't want to spoil what little time remained by having her slap him in the face and reject him. She'd just said they were friends. It might be all she would ever want from him.

"That's very nice of you, Berny. Are you sure you want to go to all that trouble?"

"It will be a joy to cook for you," Bernadette assured him with a happy smile. "You weren't going to have guests, were you?"

He shook his head. "No. What time should I come over?"

"Oh, come over as soon as you get up," she told him. "We'll spend the whole day together and you can help me open my gifts."

His blue eyes grew soft as he looked down at Bernadette's face. "You're making this Christmas very special for me, Bernadette."

"It's been special for me, too, Nick. Very special." It was the most she would allow herself to say. Even though she would have liked to have said how much she hoped they would be together like this next year.

The party was turning into a long one. Everyone was enjoying themselves and no one wanted to go home. Nick and Bernadette danced endlessly. Bernadette was glad because it gave her the chance to be in his arms. Nick was glad because it gave him an excuse to hold her.

They were one of the last couples to leave the building.

"So, how do you like partying now?" she asked through chattering teeth.

"It was far nicer than I expected. And I liked your friends, Berny." He backed the car out of the parking space and headed toward the exit.

Bernadette said, "They liked you, too, Nick. I could tell. They still regarded you with a bit of awe, but they liked you."

Nick smiled in the darkness. "There you go putting me behind my desk again."

"It's a habit," she reasoned. "You were Mr. Atwood for two years. And you're still my boss."

"I'd rather you think of me as your partner," he said in a low voice.

Bernadette was surprised by his words. Or maybe it was his intimate tone that had her thinking twice. It made her realize how much she wanted to be his partner in love and life, not just in the workplace. She wondered how he would react if she told him that. He'd probably be stunned, but then he'd quickly collect himself and remind her of Doreen.

"Berny! I'm afraid we're in trouble!"

The alarm in Nick's voice jolted her out of her thoughts.

"What's the matter?"

"Ice! Look out the window," he told her.

Their car was just leaving the shelter of the underground parking area, and Bernadette leaned forward to peer out the windshield. Everything was glistening with a coat of clear ice at least an inch thick. Already there were cars stalled along the street.

"I thought we might find a little snow when we left the party, but not this!" She groaned. "What are we going to do? Do you think we can make it home?"

"I don't know. Let me see if I can pull out onto the main street."

Bernadette clutched her coat tightly around her and watched tensely as Nick allowed the car to roll forward. The street was covered with a solid sheet of ice, reducing traction to nil.

The car had slipped and slid for three blocks when Nick finally said, "Berny, I think the best thing to do is to try to make it to my house, since it's closer than your apartment. We'll figure out something once we get there."

"I'm agreeable to anything that will get us off the streets," she quickly told him.

What would normally have taken them five minutes to drive now took thirty-five minutes. Bernadette was greatly relieved when Nick gently braked the car to a stop in front of a massive stone house.

"The driveway has a pretty steep incline. I think I'd better leave the car here."

She nodded. "I think you're right. Maybe no one will skid into it here on the street," she added hopefully.

Nick came around to help her out of the car. She reached for her handbag and took a tight hold on his arm with her free hand. The ground was terribly slick, making walking a dangerous task, particularly in high heels.

The freezing rain was still falling steadily. Bernadette's hair was wet by the time they reached the house.

"Oh, this feels wonderful," Bernadette exclaimed when Nick opened the door and she felt a rush of warm air. After shaking some of the moisture from her hair she glanced around to see they were in a large foyer. "Does your help live in?"

"No, they come in around six every morning. But since tomorrow is Christmas Day they'll be home with their own families. Come on, let's go into the great room. It should be warmer there," he said, taking her by the arm.

Bernadette was expecting the house to be austere and formal and was pleasantly surprised to find it had a warm charm instead.

The great room was long and filled with comfortable stuffed furniture. A stone fireplace stood at one end. Windows formed most of the wall that looked out over the front grounds. Standing near the middle of the windows was a huge Colorado blue spruce, its boughs weighed with brilliant tinsel, lights, shiny balls and what seemed like hundreds of candy canes.

"Oh, Nick, what a magnificent tree!"

"Do you like it?"

Her eyes on the tree, she walked toward it. "It's absolutely beautiful!" She turned to Nick. "Did you trim it yourself?"

He shook his head. "I've never trimmed a tree in my life," he admitted. "I wouldn't know where to start. My housekeeper did this one. It's the first tree that's been in this house for years."

"Oh, surely not! That's terrible, Nick. How did you go through past Christmases without a tree?"

He shrugged. "I never do much celebrating over the holidays. But this year..."

But this year Doreen was coming for a visit, she silently finished his sentence. Bernadette couldn't bear to think of it. She walked over to the windows, struggling to force her attention on the weather. "It looks like the rain is still falling. If this keeps up everything will come to a halt," Bernadette commented.

"I hope all the holiday travelers have reached their destinations by now. The interstate highways will be deadly soon."

Bernadette looked over her shoulder at Nick. "I was beginning to wonder if we'd make it even this far. I suppose it would be foolish to try to drive to my house."

"I'm afraid so, Berny."

Her brows drew together as she considered all options. "I have a friend who has a four-wheel drive. She'd come after me if I called and asked her to."

Nick joined Bernadette by the windows. "I don't think that would be wise, either, Berny. Even though she has four-wheel drive, there just isn't any traction on this ice. Snow would be a different matter, but unfortunately it looks like we're in the middle of an ice storm instead of a snowstorm."

Bernadette knew he was right. It would be insanity for anyone to try to travel tonight. "I suppose this means you're stuck with me."

He grinned at her. "I wouldn't say stuck, Berny. Besides, we planned to spend tomorrow together anyway. We'll just be in a different house."

"Oh, but my turkey!" Bernadette wailed, suddenly remembering the bird she'd taken such pains picking out at the supermarket. "And all the things I'd planned to cook. What will I do about them?"

"We'll raid the pantry. Surely Mrs. Gaines, my housekeeper, has something suitable stocked away." He touched her forearm. "Come on, why don't we go to the kitchen and I'll make a pot of coffee. I don't know how to cook, but I do know how to make coffee."

She smiled at him and felt her mood lifting. At least the storm was giving her more time with Nick than she'd first anticipated. "That sounds lovely."

They walked out of the room, down a short hallway and through a doorway on the left, which led to a huge dining area. At the back of it was a door leading into the kitchen.

"What a room! This is probably bigger than my whole apartment!" Bernadette exclaimed once Nick had switched on the overhead lights. Shiny stainless steel fixtures and blue tile gleamed spotlessly. Copper pans hung from a long work island. At one end of the room was a wooden table with a bench pushed behind it.

Bernadette sat down on the bench and watched Nick as he assembled the makings for the coffee.

"I can't imagine you living alone in this huge place. Do you like it?"

Nick switched on the cold water tap and thrust the percolator beneath it. "Outside of my college days, I've always lived in this house. I wouldn't know what it would be like not to."

Bernadette let her eyes travel around the room. "Well, I suppose it would be nice if you had a wife and children. There'd be plenty of space," she mused aloud. "But I'd get lost here all by myself."

Nick plugged in the percolator, then glanced over to Bernadette. "I always bring work home from the office. But the house *is* quiet," he agreed, thinking it always reminded him of a tomb after he'd spent a day working with Bernadette.

The percolator began to make a swooshing noise. Bernadette glanced from it to Nick. For some reason she felt awkward now that they were alone in his home. The idea that they would be alone all night and tomorrow kept going round and round in her mind. Could she trust herself not to blurt out her feelings for him?

If she had any sense she would use this opportunity to her advantage, she thought. But she wasn't that kind of woman, and she never wanted to do anything that might make Nick lose his respect for her.

"Is this where your parents lived, too?" she asked.

He nodded. "Dad had this house built for my mother when they first came to Oklahoma. They did a lot of socializing and Mother wanted plenty of grandeur and space. Since my parents went to California, however, I've exchanged most of the furnishings for something more relaxed. The last time they came for a visit, Mother clucked her tongue at it all. I had to remind her that it was *my* house now."

Bernadette's smile was knowing. "Sometimes we have to do things like that. But I think it's all very beautiful. I wouldn't change a thing," she insisted.

"And it's much warmer than outside in an ice storm," he added wryly.

Bernadette laughed. "Yes, much warmer."

"Would you like to look in the pantry now while the coffee is brewing?"

"Sure. Lead the way."

The pantry turned out to be almost as large as the kitchen itself. Foodstuff of all sorts lined the endless rows of shelves. There were also two deep freezers where meat and frozen goods were kept.

"Nick, here's a duck," Bernadette said, pulling a package from one of the freezers. "Would you care for roast duck tomorrow?"

"Roast duck is one of my favorites," he replied. "Do you think you can find the things you need to go with it?"

"Nick! You could probably start a restaurant with all this food. I'm sure I'll find everything I need."

Nick carried the bird back into the kitchen to thaw. By now the coffee was ready and he poured them each a mugful.

Deciding it might be wise to check the television for a weather report, they carried their coffee back to the great room. Bernadette kicked off her high heels and curled up on the couch while Nick switched on the TV.

A program came on, but a weatherman interrupted the show almost instantly. The forecast was grim— more precipitation, with the temperatures plunging even lower tonight. The highway patrol was warning everyone to stay off the streets unless it was an extreme emergency.

"It doesn't sound too promising, does it?" Bernadette said, once the station switched back to regular programming.

"No. But it shouldn't be a problem for us. Tomorrow is a holiday so we don't have to worry about getting to the office. And, as you can see, I have plenty of space. You can choose any bedroom you like."

"Goodness, I haven't stopped to think that I have nothing with me. No clothes or toothbrush," Berny said as Nick joined her on the couch.

"There are new toothbrushes in every bathroom. And you could probably wear something of mine if necessary," he said.

"Like pajamas?"

Nick's face suddenly turned a shade darker. "I—sorry, Berny, I don't sleep in pajamas."

Bernadette felt a warm blush creep across her cheeks. She should have stopped to think that he might sleep in the raw. Now that she knew, the idea made a sensual picture in her head, one that was difficult to shake away.

The corners of her lips tilted upward sexily. "Oh well, an old shirt will be fine," she quickly assured him.

Nick's blue eyes glinted with a spark she'd never seen before. "I have plenty of those," he said, then added with a wry grin, "or at least I did until I gave them to the Salvation Army."

Bernadette was suddenly aware of the comical side of it all and she laughed out loud. In a matter of seconds Nick had joined her.

The tinkle of her laughter filled the quiet room, and as he looked at her sparkling blue eyes and smiling face, Nick decided that she was what had always been lacking in his home. Her presence made it a warm, joyous place.

Nick took a sip of coffee, then said, "I take it your mother flew to Taos. I'd hate to think of her traveling on the highway in this weather."

Bernadette nodded while reaching up to undo the red lace from her hair. "Yes. She'll fly back Monday night. Do your parents ever join you for Christmas?"

His eyes dropped from her face and down to his coffee mug. "No. It's too cold here in December for Mother's health."

Bernadette decided that his parents lived a life completely separate from their son's. It made Nick seem so totally alone, and she longed to tell him that no matter how things went with Doreen, she would always be here for him.

"What about your father, Berny? Does he ever come home for Christmas?" Nick asked.

Bernadette frowned and pushed her fingers through the tousled blond curls around her face.

"Occasionally. I'd just as soon he not, anyway," she admitted, her voice losing its happy lilt.

Nick's brows lifted. "Why is that?"

She shrugged and found she was unable to meet Nick's gaze. "He usually has a woman with him, and it . . . just makes things uncomfortable."

Nick was silent for a moment. "For you or your mother?" he finally asked.

Berny looked up to meet his gaze. "It doesn't seem to bother my mother. But it bothers me," she reluctantly admitted.

Nick's eyes softened as he watched a hint of unhappiness shadow her face. He was surprised at her attitude. He'd never seen her react to anything in this downcast way. "Why?"

Her lips tightened a fraction. "Nick, he's my father! Mother should be the woman by his side, not someone else!"

His hand reached out and curled comfortingly over her shoulder. "Berny, don't you think your mother is the one who should decide that sort of thing?"

Bernadette sighed. It always angered her when she thought about her father's betrayal, and she didn't want to become angry and spoil this special time with Nick. "Mother didn't have a choice. My dad was the one who chose to leave the marriage," she told him sadly.

Nick's head shook with regret. "I'm sorry, Berny. I shouldn't have pried."

Her head was still bent down, and he watched her fingers nervously pleat the material of her dress. "You weren't prying, Nick. Anyway, you couldn't have known."

"Do you hate your father?" he asked. It astonished Nick to think that Bernadette could harbor such an emotion inside her. She seemed so full of compassion, understanding and a zest for life that bubbled behind her blue eyes.

Bernadette's eyes jerked around to his. "Sometimes I try to hate him. When I think of how he lied to my mother about all the times he was actually with another woman."

In all the time that Nick had known Bernadette, he'd never seen such a stricken look on her face. She was always such a positive, happy person that it was difficult to imagine any kind of sadness ever entering her life.

Quickly he closed the small gap between them, put his arms around her and gently guided her head to his shoulder. "I'm sure that your father loves you, Berny. It wasn't your fault that your parents parted."

Bernadette pressed her cheek against his neck. It was sweet and reassuring to be held by Nick. He was like no one else. "My mother is beautiful and kind, Nick. I've never been able to understand why Daddy wasn't satisfied with only her."

Nick's fingers threaded through her hair, then gently rubbed her scalp. "I expect it had nothing to do with your mother, Berny. There's probably something missing inside your dad that makes him search for someone new, someone to fill the void. I think the best thing you could do now is hope he finds it.''

She lifted her head to look at him. Doubt and questions filled her eyes. "Is that what you truly think, Nick?''

His eyes caressed her face. "You can't put your family back as it was before," he said. "And people sometimes need to be forgiven for their shortcomings. Somehow I feel it would be worse if your father had stayed and pretended to be happy.''

Bernadette slowly digested his words. "I suppose that would be lying, too," she murmured.

Her lashes fell against her cheeks, and Nick felt his self-control slipping farther away.

"Pretending, lying, it's all the same to a man," she went on.

Nick froze inside. "Hey, I'm a man, remember?'' he voiced lightly.

Suddenly she smiled up at him, and Nick could see trust written all over her face. He wanted to groan aloud.

"Sorry, Nick. I didn't mean you. I know that you would never lie to anyone. Especially someone you love.''

What had he done to himself, he wondered desperately. How could all this possibly end?

He couldn't find it in himself to hold her gaze. "No. I would never do that," he said quietly.

Chapter Eight

Bernadette suddenly pulled away from him. "My goodness," she said, forcing some cheer back into her voice, "this is Christmas Eve. We shouldn't be talking about such somber things. Tell me what you've gotten for Christmas so far."

Nick reached for his coffee. He was relieved to see her mood lift. He never wanted Bernadette to be sad about anything. "Sooner gave me a big bonus. And my parents gave me a nice piece of stock."

Money, Bernadette thought. She'd agonized over what to get Nick. Last Christmas she'd gotten him an impersonal pen set—a typical gift for a secretary to give her boss. But this Christmas was different, and she wanted his gift to be different, too. However, since Nick was wealthy and could buy himself anything, she'd finally decided that the best gift would be something personal that would fit within her moderate budget. Now she was glad that she'd purchased a pullover sweater for him.

Joyce would probably tell her that a piece of clothing was too personal, but Bernadette didn't care if it was. In fact, she'd decided that she wanted Nick to know that she looked at him as a man, as someone she'd grown very close to.

Bernadette smiled at his serious expression. "No cigars, liquor or silk ties?"

Nick returned her smile, thinking he'd like to tell her that her company this Christmas was the best gift of all. "Well, I think there are a few of those in the office that I haven't opened yet," he said. "So, your turn. What have you gotten so far?"

"Nick!" she scolded with a laugh, "I don't cheat. I wait to open all of my gifts on Christmas Day." Her fingers suddenly went to the jeweled reindeer pinned to her breast. "Except for your gift, Nick," she said, her voice softening. "I'll wear it every Christmas."

Nick hoped that she'd still feel that way once the holidays were over.

"You'll just have to wait to get your gift from me," she went on. "Since it's at home under my little tree."

"You shouldn't have bothered getting me anything, Berny," he said truthfully.

Bernadette sipped the last of her coffee, then said, "I know. You're one of those men who has everything. But I happen to think you deserve a gift anyway," she teased.

Nick's eyes slid over to the decorated spruce and all the gifts beneath it. Bernadette followed his gaze and felt her spirits fall flat. All the gifts she'd helped him choose for Doreen were stacked beneath the tree.

She tried her best to sound casual. "I hope I steered you right where Doreen's gifts are concerned. It would have helped if I'd had the chance to meet her."

Nick had to clear his throat before he could make his vocal chords work. "Don't worry about it, Berny. Your taste was excellent. I believe she'll like all of them."

Bernadette had an impulsive urge to reach over and shake him. Can't you see I care for you more than any woman you've ever known, she wanted to cry out. Instead she asked abruptly, "Are you sleepy? I don't want to keep you up."

He shook his head, wondering if the wicked thoughts that were dancing across his mind were written on his face. "No. Are you?"

"No," she answered, "the caffeine from the coffee has revived me."

Restlessly she rose to her feet and walked over to the windows. The glass was fogged over. Bernadette lifted her hand and swiped a circling motion over one of the panes. Pressing her nose against the window, she strained to see out into the blackened night. It looked as though sleet and freezing rain were still falling. Already the trees near the house were bending under the heavy weight of the ice.

"Has it stopped?" Nick asked.

She shook her head. "Not at all. In fact, I think it might be worsening."

Turning away from the window, she crossed back to the couch.

"Are you hungry?" Nick asked once she'd taken her seat beside him.

"I couldn't eat anything after all that food at the party."

"That's the way I feel," Nick told her.

She leaned her head back against the couch and settled her eyes on the television set. Why couldn't she get her mind on something, anything except the need to be near Nick, the need to have him love her?

"It looks like an old movie is coming on," she said. "I suppose we could watch it."

"You like old movies?"

She nodded. "Especially if they were made in the forties or fifties."

Nick went over and turned up the volume of the set. After he'd taken his seat beside her once again, he took Bernadette's hand in his. "So do I," he said. "Especially if I have a hand to hold."

Had he ever sat in a darkened theater and held a date's hand? she wondered. A month earlier she would have never been able to visualize her stern boss doing anything so romantic. But now she could easily picture it. And the woman she pictured at his side was herself. "Everything is better when you have a hand to hold," she replied, giving his fingers a squeeze.

The black and white movie was one of those detective stories that were so popular in the fifties. The plot was very complicated and the acting superb. For an hour Bernadette was lost in the movie, but then her eyelids began to droop. Before long, she was sound asleep, her head nestled on Nick's shoulder.

Afraid he would disturb her if he moved, Nick stayed where he was and tried to keep his mind on the movie. After a while he gave up the effort and allowed himself to watch Bernadette as she slept. It was a treasure to hold her in his arms. It reminded him how good, how sweet life would be if she were always here with him.

Bernadette woke slowly. Little by little she realized that the front of her was warm, but her back was cold. She was also lying in a twisted position and whatever was beneath her definitely wasn't a mattress!

Her eyelids fluttered open and her breath drew in softly. She was lying on top of Nick. Her palms were flattened against his chest, her cheek nestled between them.

She gasped softly and lifted her head. The sound must have woken him up because he opened his eyes at the same time she was trying to decide how to extricate herself from his hold around her waist.

"Berny?"

"Nick."

"You fell asleep," he whispered.

"I think you must have fallen asleep, too," she murmured.

Bernadette wondered why they were talking about something they were both already aware of. And why couldn't she find it in her to move away from him?

"I—I should—" she began but stopped when Nick's hands tightened on her waist. The shock of waking up in his arms was leaving her and being replaced by something altogether different.

This was the man she loved, and it was wonderful to touch him this way. He felt deliciously warm and strong and masculine. It was impossible not to want to kiss him and feel his hands move against her.

"Berny, I—"

She heard a thread of impatience in his voice, but before she could wonder about it, Nick pulled her head down to his. He captured her lips with a fierceness that excited her drowsy senses. Her fingers curled on his chest and her mouth parted for his.

This evidence of Bernadette's desire made Nick groan, and he slid his hands down her back to press her even closer. She tasted sweet and exciting. And even though Nick knew he should end the embrace, he found it was impossible to make himself separate her from him. He'd loved her and had wanted her for so long and now here she was, kissing him as though she really meant it, as though she really cared for him.

Bernadette wriggled closer against him. Nick tightened his hold and shifted her so that she was pressed between him and the couch.

By now Bernadette was hardly aware of where she was. Nick's touch and taste were causing her to lose all sense of reasoning. Her hands explored the muscles of his back, then slipped up his neck, and her fingers tangled with his dark hair. When his tongue pushed between her teeth, she moaned softly in her throat and met the warm, intimate invasion with her own tongue.

Unwittingly her legs wrapped around his in a silent gesture of need. Her breathing grew shallow and rapid. She'd never wanted any man this way! The physical need for him to make love to her was burning throughout her, taking complete hold of her mind.

"Berny, ah, Berny..." Nick's voice was thick and husky, making Bernadette wonder if he wanted her as badly as she wanted him. But that would be impossible, she thought. She loved Nick, whereas he was waiting for another woman to come to town!

The realization brought a sweeping chill through her. It doused the flames of desire that, a moment earlier, had been threatening to get out of control. She couldn't do this! Not when Doreen was the woman he really wanted!

"Nick! I—"

Nick could feel her stiffen and begin to pull away from him. Reluctantly he raised his head. Her face was twisted in anguish, which confused him greatly. A moment ago she had been melting in his arms. Now she looked as though she wanted to burst into tears. What had he done? "Berny, what's wrong? Did I hurt you?"

Yes, but not the way you think, she wanted to say. Instead, she shook her head in silent misery.

Nick levered himself away from her. Bernadette immediately scrambled to a sitting position and pushed down the hem of her dress from where it had ridden up around her thighs.

Tentatively he reached out and touched her forearm. "Berny, I didn't mean to—I—" Damn it! How was he going to explain his feelings without letting her know he'd been lying about Doreen all this time? He'd seen the bitter look on her face when she'd spoken of her father. He wasn't ready for that!

"Don't say anything, Nick," she murmured, her head bent. "I'm not blaming you. I just forgot all about Doreen and—"

She didn't go on and Nick let out a frustrated sigh.

"I guess I forgot about her, too," he said, raking his fingers through his tousled hair.

Dear Lord, he was aching to pull her back into his arms. Maybe he should make a confession here and now, he thought. They were in the middle of an ice storm, so at least she couldn't run away from him, although she could lock herself in one of the bedrooms.

"Nick! Something is wrong!"

He swallowed with anticipation, seeing her head jerk upward. "What do you mean?"

"The lights. The TV. They're off, and it's cold in here."

He'd been so afraid she was going to start into him about Doreen that it took a minute for him to realize she was talking about something entirely different.

"The power has gone off," he said with grim realization. "I'll check the fuse box, but I'm willing to bet the ice has broken down power lines somewhere near."

He rose to his feet. "Do you have a flashlight handy?" she asked.

"In the kitchen," he answered, then glanced over his shoulder to notice she was following him. "Maybe you should stay here, Berny. You might trip over something in the darkness. I wouldn't want you hurt for anything."

The concern in his voice warmed her. Doreen had invaded and ruined their passionate embrace, but Bernadette wasn't going to let the other woman ruin everything. Nick did care about her, even if it was only as a close friend.

"I might be able to help," she insisted. "Don't worry about me."

"Here, take my arm. It's pitch-black in here. It looks as though the street lamps and yard lights are knocked out also."

He began to move slowly across the room and Bernadette clung tightly to his arm. "You wouldn't happen to have a backup generator for this place, would you?"

"Afraid not," he answered regretfully. "To make matters worse the heating system runs partially from electricity. It will be freezing in here shortly if the power isn't restored soon."

They made it to the kitchen without any major bumps or breaks. Nick fished a flashlight from a cabinet and Bernadette felt better about things when the yellow orb of light illuminated part of the room.

"The fuse box is down in the basement," he told her. "Want to stay here or come along?"

"I don't want to stay here in the dark," she assured him.

Nick opened a door to reveal cement steps leading down. They went down to the basement, which was freezing cold and filled with an odd assortment of objects.

While Nick examined the fuse box, Bernadette hugged herself for warmth and glanced around. Several pieces of furniture stood shrouded beneath white sheets. If Bernadette had been the spooky sort, she would have found it easy to imagine the place was filled with ghosts. However, in one corner, she spotted a stack of firewood and her spirits lifted.

"Nick, is this firewood for the fireplace in the great room?"

He turned away from the electrical box and aimed the flashlight in her direction.

"Yes, it is."

"Then we can build a fire?"

"Great idea, Berny. At least that will keep one room bearable." He moved over a stack of crates toward Bernadette. "There's nothing wrong with the fuses. It has to be the ice," he told her.

"Well, then, let's carry up some wood," she suggested. "The fire will also provide us with a bit of light."

"Mrs. Gaines has put out several candles for Christmas decorations. We can light those, also."

They both loaded their arms with firewood and carefully made their way up the stairs to the great room. It was only a few minutes before Nick had a fire crackling merrily in the hearth.

Bernadette stood as close to the flames as possible. Now that the heating system was off, she wished she had worn something other than the white dress she had on. Its short skirt was doing little to keep her warm.

"This feels wonderful," she said as the heat from the flames began to seep through her clothing.

Nick, who was standing near the windows looking out at the ice-covered grounds, turned and gave her a wry smile. "This is one Christmas Eve I'll never forget."

Bernadette wondered if it was because of the storm or because of her earlier behavior. Her cheeks still burned when she thought of how wantonly she'd behaved in his arms. He was probably thinking she was one of those women who made a practice of stealing men from other women.

It was humiliating to Bernadette, but it was even more painful. "Nor will I," she admitted.

He walked back to her and the fireplace. "I'm sorry all of this has happened, Bernadette. I wanted you to enjoy tonight. Now here you are in a dark, freezing house."

"It's not your fault, Nick. Besides, I'm sure the power company will have the electricity restored by morning. There's nothing else we can do tonight anyway except sleep."

Nick could think of lots of things he'd rather be doing than sleeping, but he forced his mind away from those thoughts. He'd probably already lowered her opinion of him. She was probably already thinking he was one of those men who took advantage of any female who was in close range.

Nick hated the idea of presenting that kind of image to Bernadette and wondered if there was anything he could say to explain himself without making things worse.

"Berny, I hope—" He stopped and ran his hands tiredly over his eyes.

"Are your contacts bothering your eyes, Nick?" she asked with sudden concern.

He shot her a quizzical look. He'd forgotten he was even wearing the things. "No. No, not at all. I just—" Sighing, he reached out and gently touched her shoulder. "I just hope you're not angry because of—of what happened earlier. It wasn't planned, Berny. If I offended you—"

Bernadette couldn't bear to hear him apologizing for something she'd encouraged. "No, you didn't," she quickly interjected. "I—I was doing my share of—of kissing." She felt her throat tighten as she scanned his features. "I was afraid you were thinking badly of me," she confessed in a husky whisper.

"Why?" he asked, surprised.

She pulled her eyes away from him. "Doreen."

The one word was all she needed to say. He dropped his hand from her shoulder.

"I was thinking you'd think the same of me," he confessed. "That I was fickle."

Bernadette hadn't stopped to consider his part in things. Even so, she could never think of him as fickle. She'd never seen him with a woman, much less changing from one to the next. "No, of course I don't think that," she assured him.

Nick felt some of the tension drain from him. "You're a very attractive, desirable woman," he said, "and I'm not blind." Hell, Nick, you were in the dark! You're making things even worse.

She looked back at him and a smile crept across her face. "You're an attractive man, too, Nick. I guess I'm not as immune to men as I always like to believe I am."

"I'm glad," he said, then hastily added, "I mean, I'm glad you're not angry with me."

"Well, we were under unusual circumstances," she reasoned, her cheeks growing warm at the memory of it all.

"Yes. Very unusual," he agreed in a brusque, businesslike voice.

Standing there so close beside him in the darkness, Bernadette had the greatest urge to throw her arms around him. She wanted more than anything to tell him that she loved him and wanted to make him forget all about Doreen. It was an effort to keep her hands at her sides.

"Well," she said on a long breath. "Shall we go to bed?"

Nick cleared his throat. "Er, ah, Berny, I think that might be the wrong thing to do."

Her eyes widened as she peered up at his face. "I didn't mean together, Nick!"

"No, of course you didn't," he said quickly. "I just meant that since the heat is off, the bedrooms will be freezing. It might make more sense if we stayed here by the fire."

"Oh. Yes, you're probably right. I keep forgetting all the complications a power outage can cause."

"You can take the couch and I can sleep on the floor in front of the fireplace."

Bernadette shook her head. "There's no way I'll allow you to sleep on the floor in this kind of weather. You'll wind up with pneumonia."

"I'll use lots of blankets," he assured her.

"There'll be a draft on your face," she said and walked over to the couch. "Look, there's enough room for you and me both. I'll get at one end and you can have the other. It's the sensible thing to do."

Nick had doubts about the sensibility of it. He didn't know if he could trust himself to be that close to her again and not touch her. "I don't really think—"

Before he could say more Bernadette grabbed hold of one end of the couch and began to tug. "Come here and help me get it closer to the fire," she told him. "That way we'll both stay warm."

Nick knew it would be pointless to argue any further with her about it. As a sign of surrender, he walked over to help her.

Thirty minutes later, Bernadette, dressed in one of Nick's white shirts, was snuggled beneath a thick layer of blankets on one end of the couch. Nick, covered by different blankets, was on the other. As a concession to Bernadette's presence, he'd put on sweatpants.

Earlier they had blown out all the candles and now the room was completely dark, except for the small area that was illuminated by the fire. Across the room, sleet continued to pelt the windows.

"Nick," Berny said drowsily as she stared into the flames of the fire, "two years ago when I became your secretary, did you ever think we'd be sleeping together?"

Nick was lying on his back, staring up at the ceiling. He couldn't decide whether to groan with frustration at her question or laugh at the craziness of it all. Finally he did the latter. "No, Berny, I didn't think things would...wind up like this." He wasn't going to tell her he'd dreamed about "sleeping" with her from the first moment he saw her.

Bernadette chuckled as she remembered how stern and businesslike he'd been in those days. "No, I guess you didn't. Nick?"

"Yes."

"Are you sorry you began all these lessons?"

He was silent for a few moments. Bernadette lifted her head and looked down the long length of the couch to see if he'd fallen asleep.

"Of course I'm not sorry," he answered finally. "Dad always said learning was the best part of living. In this case it couldn't be truer. I've enjoyed each moment with you, Berny."

Bernadette let her head fall back against the pillow. She was suddenly happy and content. If he enjoyed being with her, maybe he'd find that once Doreen arrived, Doreen no longer interested him. It was a thought to hold on to.

"So have I, Nick. I'm glad you chose me for a teacher."

The darkness hid Nick's mouth as it curved into a faint smile. He decided for the next few days he'd better do some hard praying. "Believe me, Berny, I knew what I was doing when I chose you."

Chapter Nine

Merry Christmas, Berny."

Bernadette slowly opened her eyes. Nick was standing over her, a cup of steaming coffee in his hand.

She rubbed her eyes and swept back the tangle of blond curls around her face. "It's already morning?" she asked in wonder. It felt as if she'd only just closed her eyes.

Nick chuckled. "Yes, and the freezing rain has stopped. Here," he said, holding the coffee out to her, "this is for you. And there's one of my robes, if you'd like to put it on."

She saw that he'd draped a plaid flannel robe over the back of the couch. Bernadette reached for it and flung aside the blankets.

Surveying her long, lovely legs beneath the tails of his white shirt, Nick was amazed at himself. Any man who could sleep beside Bernadette without making love to her had to be made of steel, or crazy. He didn't know which choice to pin on himself.

"You're so thoughtful, Nick," she said quickly, belting the robe around her slim waist. Once she had it safely secured, she reached to take the coffee from him.

"I'm sorry I'm not a cook, or I would have already made breakfast," he told her.

Nick had built up the fire. The flames were sending out rays of delicious heat. Bernadette sat on the floor near the hearth and sipped the coffee.

"This is wonderful. And *I'll* make us breakfast. It's the least I can do for causing you trouble."

"Trouble?" he asked.

She smiled at him, and Nick was certain he'd never seen any woman look so beautiful.

"I took up all that space on the couch that you could have used."

His returning smile was wry. "I'm always alone in this house, Berny. It's nice to have you here."

Bernadette's heart warmed to his words. "And it's Christmas!" She glanced around her and noticed the lights were on. "The power has been restored, too!"

He nodded. "The TV woke me up when it played the national anthem."

"Do you have any idea how the streets are?"

"The radio said very hazardous. But fair weather is supposed to be here by this afternoon. By tonight I should be able to drive you back to your apartment."

"There's no hurry. After all, there's a duck waiting for me to cook for you," she reminded him.

After Bernadette drank her coffee she went to dress. The only makeup she had with her was a tube of lipstick and a powder compact. But after she'd brushed her hair into order, she felt she was presentable.

The two of them decided to have a light breakfast of toast and jam and save room for the duck. They spent the rest of the morning playing chess by the fire and listening to Christmas carols on the radio.

Nick's parents called at midmorning to wish him a Merry Christmas. Bernadette figured her mother would try to reach her at her apartment. Bernadette hoped she wasn't worried when she didn't get an answer. There was no way her mother could know that she had been stranded here at Nick's house.

When it came time to prepare dinner, Nick helped Bernadette find all the utensils, spices and other fresh food she would need.

While Bernadette got the duck ready to roast, she put Nick to work chopping celery and oranges for the stuffing and doing general tasks that didn't require cooking skills. She greatly enjoyed his company in the kitchen, and she teased him about their roles being reversed and that she was now the boss.

Both she and Nick sniffed appreciatively when the duck with orange stuffing could be smelled baking in the oven.

"My poor turkey must be feeling pretty lonely about now," Bernadette said. "But the duck smells heavenly."

"Perhaps we could have the turkey for dinner on New Year's Day," Nick suggested. "That is, if you'd still like to have me over?"

Bernadette shot him a strange look. "Nick, have you forgotten the party and Doreen?"

Nick felt himself blushing. If he wasn't careful he was going to wind up making one too many slips. If

Bernadette figured this thing out before he planned to tell her, he knew it would be disastrous. "Yes. I guess I had forgotten."

"I don't imagine you'd want to bring her over?" Bernadette felt compelled to ask. She wanted Nick to know she'd love to invite him. But she didn't know about seeing him with Doreen. She really didn't think her heart could stand it.

"No!"

His outburst stunned her. Pushing her hands through her hair, she studied him through narrowed eyes. "You think if she found out we were, er, friends, it would hurt your cause?"

"Oh, definitely," he said emphatically. "In fact, I think it would ruin everything!"

The strong emotion in his voice told Bernadette that his infatuation with Doreen hadn't dimmed at all.

Bernadette turned back to the kitchen counter. What was she going to do about this? she wondered. Was she just going to stand back and let some other woman move into his life? she asked herself. Well, who's to say that Doreen will be interested? Don't kid yourself, Bernadette. The woman will take one look at Nick and lose her heart. Those emerald earrings won't hurt matters, either, she thought disgustedly. Why hadn't she been able to talk him out of those things?

"Turkey is good anytime," she told him, hoping he wouldn't detect anything amiss in her voice. "We'll make it for another day."

Nick noticed that she didn't mention Doreen or encourage his pursuit of her as she had when this had all begun. He took that as a good sign. Maybe she was beginning to want him for herself. "I'll hold you to the invitation," he said, sidling up close beside her. "Is there anything else I can do?"

Her body reacted to his nearness, and she realized her reactions were growing more intense with each physical contact with Nick. She could smell his spicy cologne and feel his shoulder brush against hers. Memory of being in his arms and kissing him flared up inside her, turning her thinking processes into one big muddle.

"I—I can't think of anything. What would you like for dessert?" she asked, not daring to look at him.

"What can you make?"

That made her laugh, and she turned her head to meet his gaze. "Oh, a few things. Apple pie, chocolate cake, bread pudding—"

"Chocolate cake," he said, not giving her a chance to go any further.

Bernadette frowned. "That's not very traditional. Especially for Christmas."

"Who's going to know? There's only you and me. Besides, Mrs. Gaines thinks I always want gourmet dishes. She never prepares plain food that simply tastes good."

"Maybe you've never told her you like plain dishes," Bernadette told him. "You have to let people know what you want."

Bernadette didn't have to tell Nick that. He was reminded of it every time he looked at her. He just wondered how she would react when he did finally tell her that she was who he really wanted.

Dinner turned out to be very enjoyable. They set the formal dining table with china and lit several candles in honor of the holiday.

Bernadette was pleased with the way her meal turned out. She was especially happy at the way Nick gazed across the table at her when they toasted dinner with a glass of wine.

The look in his eyes almost made her swear that she was the one he always wanted to be sitting across the table from. But Bernadette knew it would be foolish to hold those illusions.

As predicted, the sun came out by late afternoon, which made the streets slushy enough to be negotiable. When eight-thirty came around, Nick told her he'd better get her home before the night temperature froze the streets over again.

Once at her apartment, Nick walked Bernadette to the door and unlocked it for her.

"You have to take time to come in and open your gift," Bernadette told him as she stepped inside.

Nick didn't argue with her. He'd dreaded bringing her home. He didn't want to be away from her for any length of time. But at least he knew she would be in the office bright and early in the morning.

Bernadette made him sit on the couch before thrusting a bright red box at him.

"I know. Balloons are going to pop out of this, aren't they?"

She giggled. "I admit that sometimes I can be mischievous. But trust me, not this time."

When he found the sweater inside, she could tell he was more than surprised.

"Berny, this is very nice. But you spent too much."

She could have reminded him that the jewelry he'd given her could have probably paid for a hundred sweaters. "I know someone who has money. If I ever get down and out and need a loan I think he'd give me one.''

"With no interest," he assured her, knowing she had been referring to him.

"That's not good business," she teased and reached to lift the sweater from the box.

As she fitted it across his chest, Nick breathed in her sweet perfume and struggled to keep his hands at his sides.

"This blue is a perfect match for your eyes, especially now that you've tossed your glasses. Do you like it?''

"It's the nicest gift I've received."

She sat down beside him and carefully folded the sweater to fit back into the box. "Oh, Nick, it's just a sweater. It could hardly be compared to company stock or money."

His hand reached out and touched her forearm. Bernadette looked up into his eyes and something burgeoned inside her heart.

"It's something that can be touched and felt. It will be next to me," he said softly. "Money isn't the same."

"But you can buy any amount of sweaters you want," she said, unaware her voice was a little breathy-sounding.

"Yes, I could," he admitted. "But this one is from you. And that's what makes it special."

Bernadette was certain her heart quit beating when his hand curved against her cheek and his face lowered to hers.

His sweet, masculine and very desirable mouth moved over hers. Her hand reached out and touched his shoulder. She wanted to cling to him, to make the moment last all night. But before she had the chance to think about that, Nick was pulling away from her.

"I—I think I'd better go," he said in a husky voice.

The drowsy look in Bernadette's blue eyes made him want to grab her, carry her off and make long, delicious love to her. He had to get out of here and fast before he blew everything!

"Thank you for the sweater," he said, rising swiftly to his feet. He jerked on his coat and made it to the door before Bernadette hardly knew what was taking place.

"I'm glad you like it," she said, greatly puzzled by his behavior.

"I'll pick you up in the morning," he said, then shut the door quickly behind him.

Bemused by his quick departure, Bernadette sat down and stared at the door. He was such a contradiction at times, she thought. He said and did things like a man in love. But how could that be? The woman he loved was in New York.

A knock suddenly sounded on the door. Thinking it was Nick returning, she hurried over to open it. Lawrence stood on the small porch, his face beaming from ear to ear.

"Hi, Berny! It's about time you got home."

"Come in, Lawrence. And merry Christmas to you, too."

He gave her a sheepish grin. "Merry Christmas, Berny."

She reached out and tweaked his cheek. "Come on over to the couch and tell me all about it."

"All about what?"

Bernadette looked at him impatiently. "What you got for Christmas, Lawrence."

"Oh, lots of things. I was really surprised because Mom kept telling me I'd been awfully rotten the last two weeks."

"Sounds like you came out of it pretty lucky," Bernadette said, trying to hide her amusement.

"Sure did," Lawrence said with a smug grin. "I even got an electronic basketball game. Will you play with me, Berny? Now?"

"I'm going to shower and change my clothes, then I will. But first, do you want to help me open my gifts? I've even got one under there for you."

"Yeah!" he cried, already running to the tree.

"Something is wrong."

Bernadette shifted on her high heels and cast Joyce an innocent look. "Wrong? What do you mean?" she asked.

Joyce snorted. "It's been almost a week since our Christmas Eve party, and your strange behavior hasn't gotten any better."

"Strange behavior?" Bernadette asked, her brows lifting as she lifted the Styrofoam coffee cup to her lips.

Joyce grimaced and folded her arms across her chest. It was Friday, and the two women were taking their afternoon break along with a roomful of other workers.

"Go ahead and parrot everything I say. I won't let you skirt around the issue," Joyce told her.

Bernadette looked at her friend. "How can I skirt around the issue when I don't know what the issue is? I thought I'd been behaving in a perfectly normal way."

Joyce crumpled the empty bag of potato chips she'd been eating and tossed it in a wastebasket behind her.

"I've never seen you more *un*normal in my life," she said.

Bernadette sighed to herself. Who was she trying to fool? Not a good friend like Joyce, and certainly not herself. She was miserable and she didn't know what to do about it. Doreen and her brother were supposed to arrive tonight. She couldn't bear to think of Nick with the other woman.

"Well, I have been down a little," Bernadette mumbled. "You know what they say, that Christmas is one of the likeliest times for a person to get the blues. I suppose this year I'm struck with them."

With a great deal of concern, Joyce studied Bernadette's solemn face. "And I know exactly why you're struck. It's that boss of yours. I could tell at the party that something was going on between you two."

"Going on? That's impossible. There was nothing between us then and—"

"I know," Joyce quipped. "A piece of thread couldn't have been wedged between you two out there on the dance floor."

"Joyce, really! It wasn't—"

"It was."

"You don't know what you're talking about, Joyce. Things aren't as they appear to you."

Joyce wrinkled her nose at Bernadette. "I do have two eyes, and they're blessed with twenty-twenty vision. Mr. Atwood has come out of his cocoon, and I think you're the reason for the transformation."

"He looks fabulous, doesn't he?" Bernadette asked, deliberately ignoring Joyce's assumption.

"It's incredible. I don't think I've ever seen eyes so blue," Joyce said, then grimaced. "Darn you, Berny, why did you have to be his secretary instead of me?"

Bernadette tossed away the last of her coffee. How could she tell Joyce that Nick's change wasn't because of her? That it was an effort to garner another woman's attention? She couldn't, not without breaking her promise to Nick. "Believe me, Joyce. You have things all wrong."

"Yeah," Joyce said dryly. "That's why you look so miserable every time I mention the guy's name."

Bernadette plastered a phony bright smile on her face. "Is this better? Do I look happy now?"

"Berny, honey, you look like you could burst into tears, and I don't like it." Joyce put her arm around Bernadette's shoulder and gave it an encouraging squeeze. "You've never been serious about a man before. And in spite of the long string of boyfriends you've had, I know you're still innocent and naive about men. I'm worried about you."

Bernadette's sigh was full of frustration. "You're doing wonders at boosting my spirits."

Joyce shrugged. "I'm only warning you to be careful. I lost at the game of love. I don't want you to lose, too."

Love wasn't a game, Bernadette thought. And even if it was, she wasn't included as a player. She wasn't in the game at all. She'd started out as the teacher, but Bernadette had the feeling that she had learned more lessons than Nick. She'd learned about falling in love, and she'd learned that it was a painful process.

"Bernadette, I need for you to send Western Communications several of our coverage options. I think they're ripe for an insurance switch, and I want to make sure Sooner is their first choice."

Bernadette looked up from her typewriter to see Nick standing by her elbow. Her heart wrung into a knot as she smiled up at him. "That's a big company," she said, removing her glasses.

He smiled confidently and tapped his pen on his palm. "I like to go after the big ones. It's challenging."

Maybe that was why he was so intent on going after Doreen, Bernadette thought. Maybe it was because the woman had been impervious to him in the past.

"It would certainly be a feather in Sooner's cap to get Western Communications for a client. Not to mention yours," she told him. "I'll have the papers ready to go out in this evening's mail."

"Thank you, Berny."

He turned to go back to his office, but Bernadette's voice stopped him.

"Nick, ah, are you picking Doreen and her brother up at the airport this evening?"

He stared at her for a moment, and then his eyes darted away from hers. "No. Her brother called last night to say they'd be detained. They won't be getting here until tomorrow sometime."

"Oh. Well, you must be awfully disappointed." Saying the words had been like coughing up nails, but somehow Bernadette managed to get them out. "That means your time with Doreen will be limited."

"I certainly hope not."

The knot in her heart squeezed a bit tighter. "She will have to return to New York, won't she?" The question came out in a state of near panic.

Thoughtfully, Nick walked back to her desk. "I suppose," he said slowly. "But I'm hoping if things go well, she'll want to stay with me." That much was the truth, he defended himself.

Bernadette dropped her head and pretended to study the paper in her typewriter.

"I'm sure you'll bowl her over, Nick. You have nothing to worry about," she murmured.

He reached out and touched her shoulder. "And all because of you, Berny. What do you say we go to Ricetti's tonight? In honor of the occasion," he added.

Surprised, Bernadette lifted her eyes back up to him. "You want to go out tonight?"

"Did you have something else planned?"

She hadn't had anything planned but Nick. Couldn't he see that? "No."

"Then would you like to go? I'll even play the Boss on the jukebox for you," he said as an incentive.

She couldn't keep from smiling at that. "Of course, I'd love to go. What time should I look for you?"

"Will six-thirty be too early?"

She shook her head. "I'll be waiting."

Nick was smiling as he closed his office door behind him. Bernadette had to fight to keep from dropping her face into her hands and having a long cry.

The weather had warmed a great deal since the ice storm they'd experienced at Christmas. Bernadette dressed in jeans and black shirt, then topped it with a short leather jacket. She was ready and waiting when Nick arrived. On the way to the restaurant, Bernadette replayed the past weeks in her mind. As Nick parked his sedan in Ricetti's parking lot, Bernadette remembered when she'd insisted he loosen his tie and roll up his sleeves. He'd taken it all so good-naturedly, and she'd had such fun simply being with him.

But now all of that was going to come to a close, she thought sadly. Tomorrow Doreen would take her place. How would she be able to bear working with him every day, loving him as she did? If she lost him to Doreen, life was going to be sheer torture.

Ricetti's was as busy as the first time she and Nick went there. However, Nick found them a table at the back of the room. This time he did not feel ill at ease. Across the table he smiled at Bernadette and squeezed her hand.

"You look beautiful tonight, Berny."

Many men had complimented her on her looks and she'd taken it all in stride. Now she felt her cheeks growing warm. He'd changed her so much. "Thank you, Nick. You're looking great yourself."

His grin was lopsided as he rubbed his hand across his chest. "Do you like my sweater?"

It was the blue sweater Bernadette had given him for Christmas. She wanted to think he'd worn it just for her. "Yes," she said and smiled back at him. "I do like it."

Later, when they were eating their pizza, Bernadette found the courage to mention Doreen and the party tomorrow night. "I hope you're not worrying about it," she told him.

She felt him looking into her eyes. "No. I'm just hoping she'll understand that everything I've done, I've done for her."

There was so much emotion on his face that Bernadette felt like bursting into tears right then and there.

Instead, she waited until their night together was over. Then she cried into her pillow.

Chapter Ten

Bernadette slept late the next morning. When she did finally awaken, it was to cloudy skies and the sensation of impending doom.

Depression had left her feeling down and drained, and it was a struggle to force herself out of bed. After drinking two cups of coffee and reading the morning newspaper, she felt more human, but the depression was still with her.

This was one time in Bernadette's life when she truly felt alone. If there was someone she could confide in about this whole thing, then she might feel better. She'd certainly love to go to her mother right now and cry out the whole miserable story. But she couldn't do that to Nick. Maybe when it was all over and Nick had won Doreen, then maybe she could tell her mother about it. About how she'd foolishly fallen in love with a man who didn't know she existed other than as a friend.

It was almost noon by the time Bernadette found the initiative to get dressed. By then all she could think about was whether Doreen and her brother had arrived. She longed to call Nick and find out, but she doubted Nick would want her to. Besides, it was really none of her business now.

But it was, her heart cried. She loved the man. She couldn't just let some other woman have him! But what could she do about it?

Nothing, the more reasonable side of Bernadette's brain answered. You had your chance and you blew it. You should have made a play for the man when you had the chance.

Bernadette groaned out loud and crossed the room to look out the window. The sky was solid gray, and Bernadette was certain if she could see inside her heart right now, she would see it was exactly the same color.

You can't do this, Berny, she told herself. You can't sit in this apartment all day and think about Nick and Doreen together. Nick giving Doreen all those gifts that you chose together. Nick dancing with Doreen, holding her hand, smiling into her eyes, kissing her and—

Unable to bear the images, Bernadette hurried across to the closet and pulled a coat on over her corduroy jeans and sweater. Her mother had given her money for Christmas. She'd go shopping and buy a few pieces of clothing. Perhaps it would take her mind off Nick.

Bernadette drove to the largest shopping mall in the city and trudged up and down and in and out of every shop whose doors were open. The holiday sales were going full force. She bought two dresses and a pair of sling-backed heels. The remainder of her money she decided to save until she was in a better frame of mind. But then she wondered just when that would be. How long would it take to get over Nick? Did you ever get over loving someone?

Dusk had fallen by the time Bernadette left the mall parking lot. It frustrated her to admit she didn't feel any better now than she had this morning. She kept asking herself over and over what other women would do in her place, and she kept getting the same answer. Go to him. Tell him you love him. If he doesn't know, you'll never stand a chance.

"Hi, Berny. Where've you been?"

Bernadette jumped as Lawrence's voice sounded from behind a shrub. She shifted her purchases over to one arm and shut the car door.

"Hi, Lawrence. I've been out shopping," she said as the boy came to stand beside her.

"Going on a date tonight?"

She shook her head glumly, wishing Lawrence hadn't asked.

"What about Nick, didn't he ask you?" he continued trailing Bernadette up the sidewalk.

Her face grim, she stabbed the key into the doorknob. "No. Nick has a business party tonight."

"Oh." He looked confused, and Bernadette realized he'd never seen her acting unhappy before. "Well, whatta you gonna do tomorrow? You gonna watch the Orange Bowl? Page Sayer will be playing, and I bet you'll wanta see him."

Bernadette opened the door. "I suppose I will." To be honest, Page hadn't even crossed her mind. "You're welcome to come over and watch it with me," she told him.

This put a smile on his face. "That would be great! I will, Berny." He was already in a run back down to the sidewalk.

Turning, she called to him. "Where are you going? Aren't you coming in?"

He shook his head. "I'm supposed to be taking out the garbage. I'd better go before Mom finds out I haven't done it yet."

Bernadette waved to let him know she'd heard his loud whisper, then shut the door behind her. Without another thought, she went straight to the bathroom and stripped off her clothes.

She was going to that party and find Nick. She was going to tell him how she felt, and Doreen could go take a flying leap back to New York.

She felt much more positive now that she'd made a decision. Stepping beneath the spray of the shower, she thought she might as well make the most of it and wear one of the dresses she'd purchased today. She needed every weapon she possessed to fight Doreen.

An hour later she was driving toward downtown and the Sooner office building. A black sheath dress clung to her curves, her blonde hair was pinned up into a smooth, chic twist and long gold earrings dangled from her ears. Outwardly she looked serene and sexy, but on the inside she was a quaking mass of nerves.

First of all, an invitation was necessary to get into the party, and she didn't have one. Secondly, she had no idea what she was going to say to Nick once she did get in. She supposed that once she'd pulled him away from Doreen, the right things would come to her naturally. Or she prayed they would.

She arrived at the building and rode the elevator. She was certain it took five minutes to reach the third floor. She nervously tapped her heels and waited for the doors to open.

The board room was at the end of the corridor. She had been in it several times taking notes for Nick, but tonight she wouldn't be acting as his secretary.

Bernadette could hear the muted sound of music as she approached the double oak doors. Standing on tiptoe, she peeped through one of the small square windows on the door, then groaned at what she saw. The place was packed. It was going to be difficult spotting Nick in such a crowd.

Once inside, she found a young man attending the door.

"May I see your invitation, Miss?"

Bernadette gave him a dazzling smile. "Sorry. I don't have an invitation."

"Then I'm afraid I can't let you join the party."

"Well, actually, I don't want to join the party," Bernadette told him.

He smiled back at her in a faintly suggestive way and Bernadette knew she had him.

"Oh. Then how could I help you?"

"I'm Mr. Nicholas Atwood's private secretary. And I need to give him a message."

"A business message?" he asked, his eyes going over her black dress.

Bernadette smiled again. "Of course."

"Well, ah, just wait here for a moment and I'll see if I can locate him for you."

Bernadette nodded. "Thank you so much."

The young man left his position. Once he was out of sight Bernadette slipped into the crowd.

Ten minutes passed and she still had not found Nick. Finally she discovered Mr. Reynolds sampling a bottle of champagne. She tapped him on the shoulder.

"Well hello, Miss Baxter. Don't you look lovely tonight."

"Thank you, sir. I was wondering if you'd seen Nick?"

"Nick?"

Bernadette took a deep breath. Didn't the man know his own working partner? "Yes. Mr. Atwood."

"Atwood! Oh yes," he said, then scratched his graying head with a thoughtful expression. "I'm afraid he's already left."

Left! Bernadette gulped. This was far worse than she'd anticipated. Apparently Doreen already had ideas of her own. "Was a woman with him?"

"I can't really say. I just happened to see the back of him as he was heading out the door. A shame, too. It's turning into a great party. Care to dance, Miss Baxter? I do a mean two-step."

Bernadette smiled at him and shook her head. "Sorry, Mr. Reynolds, but I have to leave."

She wedged her way through the crowd and ran out the door and to the elevator. After the doors swished together, Bernadette leaned back against the wall and took a deep breath. What was she going to do now? She couldn't just give up.

By the time Bernadette reached her car down in the parking lot, she'd decided she would simply drive over to Nick's house. What could he do, besides be infuriated with her? If she ruined his chances with Doreen he'd never forgive her. On the other hand, if Bernadette *didn't* ruin them, she'd never forgive herself.

Nick's enormous house was as dark as midnight when Bernadette pulled up the driveway. She banged her palm against the steering wheel and cursed under her breath.

For all she knew Doreen had talked Nick into drinking champagne at the party. He wasn't accustomed to drinking, his mind would be fuzzy. The woman had probably already seduced him!

Oh, Bernadette, don't jump to wild conclusions, she berated herself. Nick is a strong, self-disciplined man. He wouldn't let himself be seduced. Unless he wanted to be, she thought with a sinking heart.

Slowly she climbed out of her car, walked over to the garage door and peered through the windows. Nick's car wasn't inside, which meant he wasn't home yet. There was nothing left for her to do now but go home. She couldn't camp here on his door step like some vagabond. The way her luck was going, a cop would probably come by and mistake her for a robber.

Throughout the drive home, Bernadette cried frustrated tears. She'd waited too late. She'd lost her chance to tell Nick she loved him.

Nick rang Bernadette's doorbell one last time. When he failed to get an answer, he turned away with a frustrated sigh. He'd never expected this to happen. He'd planned on her being home. Was she out with another man? After all, she thought he was out with Doreen. He prayed it wasn't the case.

Nick had almost reached his car to leave when Lawrence came bounding across the lawn.

"Hi, Nick. Looking for Berny?"

"Yes," he said, grateful for the boy's appearance. "Do you happen to know where she is?"

Lawrence shook his head and tossed his football up over his head. "Nope. She came in earlier but then she left again. I asked her if she had a date," he added slyly.

Nick held his breath. "Did she?"

"Nope. She said you had a business party. She seemed kinda unhappy about something."

Nick smiled at this news. "She did? That's wonderful."

Lawrence's face wrinkled with a scowl. "Are you crazy? I thought you liked Berny."

"I do like her. Very much. It's just too complicated to explain right now."

"Lawrence! Get in here. You don't have your coat on," a voice called out.

Lawrence turned to see his mother calling him from their front door. He jammed his football under his arm and trotted off. "I gotta go, Nick. See ya. I'll tell Berny you came by."

Nick waved at the boy. He was about to climb into his car when he saw Bernadette's red Z28 approaching. His heart banged against his ribs as he realized his time had just run out.

She was talking as soon as she got out of the car. "Nick! What are you doing here? The party—Doreen—?"

"Berny, you look gorgeous! Where have you been?"

Where had she been? The question stunned Bernadette. And Nick's looking her over with obvious pleasure—the sexy glint in his eyes was unmistakable—was confusing her more by the minute. "I went to the party to find you," she began.

Completely baffled, he stared at her. "Find me?"

She nodded. "You had already left. Where's Doreen?"

Taking a couple of steps toward her, Nick was sure his face had a guilty expression. "Berny, there's something I have to tell you."

"Is it about Doreen?"

Nick nodded, and Bernadette kept her eyes on his as she covered the last few steps between them. "Wait, Nick. You must let me tell you first. I thought I'd waited too late for this. Maybe I have, maybe I haven't. I just know that I can't let you go to Doreen without telling you what's in my heart."

Joy split inside Nick like a bolt of lightning. "And what is in your heart, Bernadette?" he asked in a hushed voice.

She reached for his hands and Nick's fingers clamped warmly around hers. "I know this will probably be a surprise to you, especially since I've been helping you with Doreen—" She broke off, took a deep breath and started again. "I've fallen in love with you, Nick."

Bernadette had barely gotten the words out when Nick pulled her into his arms.

"Oh, Berny, you don't know how long I've waited to hear you say those words."

The fierceness of his emotion and the crush of his embrace were turning Bernadette's mind topsy-turvy. "What do you mean? What about Doreen?"

Nick put her far enough away from him to look into her eyes. He saw love there and it gave him courage. "There is no Doreen," he said simply.

Bernadette's face jerked from side to side, making the gold earrings dance against her neck. "What do you mean 'No Doreen?' She—you—"

"I made her up. There's never been a Doreen in my life." As his hands rubbed her shoulders, he waited for her to digest his confession.

Bernadette's astonishment began to grow into hot temper. "You made her up! Nick, are you telling me this whole thing has been a farce? A joke?" she asked incredulously, her voice squeaking with fury.

His eyes pleaded with her to understand. "Not a joke, Berny. It was . . . just a plan to make you fall in love with me."

Bernadette had never been so stunned or humiliated in her life. He'd lied to her from the very beginning! Her heart felt as if he'd stomped all over it.

She opened her mouth to tell him how despicable he was, but nothing would come out.

"Berny, please let me explain."

Nick's voice jolted her back to life and she swiftly stepped around him and started up the drive. "Go away, Nick," she muttered fiercely. "Just go away."

He was there, catching her arm long before she reached the door. Tears were burning her eyes and she refused to look at him, to let him know how much he'd hurt her.

"Not until I explain," he said determinedly. "You must believe, Berny—"

Bernadette's head shot up and her bleary eyes bored into him. "Believe what? Believe what a sucker, a fool I was for ever falling for you and your . . . your lies? There's no need to worry, Nick, I believe it wholeheartedly!"

"Bernadette—"

She sniffed and jerked her arm away from his grasp with as much dignity as she could muster. "You were the one man I believed in, Nick. I trusted you always to be straight with me. I trusted you with my heart!''

"But I love you, Berny. I've loved you for two years. What was I supposed to do?"

"You could have tried telling me the truth," she shouted furiously, then turned and headed toward the steps.

Nick ran after her. "You didn't know I existed! How could I have told you something like that?"

"Why didn't you try with your mouth?"

Groaning, he said, "That would have made a big impression. I could have stood stark naked on the middle of your desk and you wouldn't have realized it was me!"

"I hardly think so. I've never seen you naked," she gritted dryly.

"Berny—"

By now she'd managed to unlock the apartment door. Stepping inside, she hissed, "I never want to see you again, Nicholas Atwood! Never!"

Nick caught the knob with his hand and stuck his foot in the door before she could slam it in his face. "You have to see me," he reminded. "I'm your boss."

Bernadette's blue eyes blazed at that. "Not for long! I'm asking for a transfer. And if I don't get one, then I'm quitting!"

With that, she stomped down on Nick's foot with a black high heel. He let out a loud howl and jerked his foot back. Before he could recover from the surprise move, she slammed the door in his face. He pounded on it with his fist. Across the street a dog began to bark loudly.

"Open the door, Berny," he pleaded with her. "You're making us both look like idiots!"

"You've already managed to do a wonderful job of that, Nick!"

"Bernadette, I love you. Don't do this to me. To us."

On the other side of the door, Bernadette covered her face with her hands as tears began to flow. "There is no us," she said, trying to choke back her sobs. "Now please leave, Nick. Please!"

It was a few moments before she heard his footsteps finally move away and eventually his car start and drive off. Bernadette thought her heart would burst with pain.

With a fresh wail of sobs, she flung herself down on the couch and wondered how she was going to exist without Nick in her life.

Bernadette slept little, if any, through the long night. She could think of nothing but Nick and the pain his deception had caused her.

Since she'd gotten up this morning, Nick had called her three times. Bernadette had hung up immediately each time, not giving him a chance to say anything. Why should she? He'd had two years to tell her how he really felt. Instead, he'd chosen to try and inveigle her with a bunch of counterfeit nonsense.

Bernadette burned with humiliation every time she thought of it and all the anguish she'd gone through imagining Nick with another woman! It was heartless of him. She could never believe in him now. Even if he did try to justify his actions by saying he loved her.

She'd seen her mother's life crumble because she'd believed in a man who mixed lies with facts. She wasn't about to put herself in that same vulnerable position.

Her determination battled with the love she felt for Nick. Tears began to fall once again as she sat at the dining table and stared out at the gray city skyline.

She was fiercely wiping away the tears when the doorbell rang. After a moment's hesitation, she decided to ignore the caller. It could be Nick and there was no way she could face him now.

"Berny? Are you okay? Where are you?"

It was Lawrence. Obviously he'd decided to stick his head in the door and yell at her. She suddenly remembered she had invited him over for the Orange Bowl game.

"In here, Lawrence. In the kitchen."

He came bounding into the room all bundled up in a new Oklahoma University sweatshirt.

"Well," she said, trying her best to muster a smile for him, "you look all ready for the game."

"Yeah! I'm ready," he exclaimed, then rounding the table, he cocked his head and gave her a guarded look. "What's the matter, Berny? Have you been crying?" The last he said in a voice that clearly stated he couldn't believe Bernadette could possibly shed a tear. She was always too happy, but she knew she didn't look happy now.

"I'm all right, Lawrence. Just a bit upset." She rubbed her puffy eyes with her fingers, feeling self-conscious at being caught crying. Especially by her little friend.

"How come?"

Bernadette's smile twisted to a rueful one. "I was slapped in the face with the truth."

"Gee, Berny, I thought we were always supposed to tell the truth." He pulled out a chair and plopped down beside her.

Bernadette sighed. "We are, Lawrence. That's just the trouble. In this case the truth came too late."

He frowned at her. "You're beatin' around the bush, Berny. Are you gonna tell me what's wrong?"

Bernadette suddenly felt the need to spill out all the things that were hurting her. Lawrence might be only a child, but he was also her friend and he cared about her.

"If you want to hear it, then yes, I'll tell you. It's Nick. Mr. Nicholas Atwood, the brilliant sales executive and the great pretender."

"You're not making much sense, Berny. Did you and Nick have a fight? I saw him last night. He was looking for you. Did you see him?"

She nodded glumly.

"You got mad at him? Gosh, Berny, you don't get mad very often. He must have done something awful."

"Awful can't begin to describe it, Lawrence," she muttered, feeling a fresh spurt of pain lance through her breast.

"Tell me about it," he pleaded, his eyes wide and expectant. "I'm old enough to understand. Please, Berny."

Bernadette told him the whole story, starting with the day Nick had asked for her help, on through to the fight they'd had last night. By the time she'd ended, fresh tears were rolling down her face.

"So you see, Lawrence," she said, dabbing at her eyes with a tissue, "Nick was lying to me all along. There was no Doreen. Now what do you think?"

"Gosh, Berny, I think Nick must love you a whole lot!"

Lawrence's words took Bernadette by complete surprise. "How do you figure that, Lawrence?"

"Well, it's pretty plain to me," he said. "'Cause I know I'd have to be crazy about a girl before I'd go to all that trouble to catch her."

Bernadette folded her arms over her breasts. Lawrence had a point, but she didn't know if she was ready to acknowledge it. Had Nick really done it all for her? Had he loved and wanted her that much?

"You have to admit, Berny, that his plan worked. You fell for him," Lawrence went on.

Bernadette grimaced. "But why did he have to use a plan at all? Why couldn't he have approached me like any normal man?"

Lawrence giggled. "Maybe he didn't feel normal around you, Berny. You havin' lots of dates and all. I bet he thought he didn't have a chance."

Chips of frozen anger began to melt and fall away from Bernadette's heart. Lawrence's words were forcing her to look at things from Nick's side. It was true that she'd had her share of boyfriends. It was also true that up until a matter of weeks ago, she'd never thought of Nick other than as a boss. Maybe he did think he needed to take drastic measures. Her heart began to lift.

"If he'd only come to me and shown me he was interested instead of using all those lies."

Lawrence watched Bernadette drum her fingers on the tabletop. "That wasn't lies, Berny. That was just pretense."

"You would say that, you're a kid."

Lawrence threw his hands up. "Gosh, Berny, I don't know what you want. Would you be happy if Doreen had been a real person?"

Bernadette's blue eyes widened in horror. "No!"

Lawrence shrugged and grinned. "Well, then, I don't see any problem."

"You don't?" she asked grimly.

"Nope. Nick loves you. You love him. If I was you, I'd go tell him so and tell him you forgive him."

"You're a typical male, Lawrence," Bernadette retorted.

Lawrence grinned and puffed out his chest. "Mom says I'm cute, too."

Bernadette found it impossible not to smile. "Yeah, squirt, you're cute, too."

"Look at it this way, Berny. The only thing Nick is really guilty of is making you fall in love with him. And you were right about him being such a smart man. I'd have never thought of anything so crafty."

Suddenly Bernadette had the urge to laugh and cry at the same time. Lawrence was right. She did love Nick, and the fact that he'd played a deceptive game couldn't change the feelings in her heart. Her mother had always stressed that to be truly happy with someone you had to trust that person in spite of everything. She had to find the courage to trust Nick now.

It took Bernadette fifteen minutes to change her clothes and drive to Nick's estate in Nichols Hills. She was so nervous when she rang the doorbell that her heart was tripping over itself.

Moments seemed to stretch as she waited for Nick to answer the bell. When the door finally creaked open, she drew in a rushed breath at the sight of him.

"Bernadette!"

"Hello, Nick."

He was so shocked to see her that he simply stared at her.

"Aren't you going to ask me in?"

Nick stepped aside. Bernadette's heels clicked on the floor as she entered the foyer. Her perfume drifted to his nostrils. Nick watched her turn to face him. She was wearing a blue turtlenecked dress that was cinched in at the waist with a wide belt. His hands ached to reach out and pull her curvy body up against his. Looking at her was wonderful, but touching her was even better, he knew. Yet he doubted she was here to allow him the pleasure of either one.

He shut the door and said, "Would you like to go into the great room?"

She nodded and preceded him into the long room.

A fire was burning on the hearth. The Christmas tree was still decorated and standing near the windows, although the lights on it weren't twinkling.

Aware that Nick was still behind her, Bernadette stopped in the middle of the room and turned to face him once again. As their eyes met, contentment poured through her heart. He loved her. It was there on his face, in his eyes. Coming to him hadn't been a mistake. It was the right thing to do.

"Happy New Year, Nick."

He looked at her quizzically. "Thank you, but I'm far from happy."

She moistened her lips, then allowed a smile to spread slowly across her face. "I'm glad that you aren't happy."

His head dropped and he raked a hand through his already tousled hair. "I'm not surprised. You made it quite clear last night how despicable you think I am."

"That's not what I meant," she said.

His head lifted. "No? Then what did you mean?"

"I'm glad that you aren't happy because that means that maybe you do really love me."

Amazed, Nick stared at her. "Of course I love you! Do you think any man would go through such an idiotic scheme if he wasn't madly in love?"

She took a few steps toward him. Her eyes softened as she spoke. "Now that I've had time to think about it, it wasn't all that idiotic. It worked, didn't it?"

He grimaced. "Not from my perspective."

"Nick, are you telling me that after going to such drastic lengths to get me that you're just giving up? I thought I taught you better than that."

He swallowed and took a step toward her. "Berny, why are you here?" he asked, his voice hoarse and expectant. "What are you trying to say?"

"I'm trying to tell you, my brilliant executive, that I love you. But you darn well better not lie to me again!"

Suddenly he was laughing and reaching for her. Bernadette stepped into his arms and buried her face on his shoulder. Hot tears oozed from beneath her closed eyelids as she clung to him.

"Oh Berny, my darling. I love you so much. I never meant to hurt you. I just want to love you. That's all I've ever wanted to do," he murmured against her cheek.

She raised her head to meet his gaze. "I love you too, Nick. After my father's leaving, I vowed never to trust another man. But you taught me there's more to love and trust than meets the eye."

He smiled down at her and reached out to wipe the tears from her cheeks. "It looks like we taught each other a lot of things. So do you forgive me? Can you trust me now? I'll never be like your father. Twenty years from now you'll know that, Berny. Are you going to marry me and give me the chance to prove it?"

She laughed with a happiness that bubbled deep inside her. "Yes, Nick! I'll marry you."

His hands cupped her cheeks and he leaned down to kiss her. Bernadette was breathless by the time he lifted his mouth from hers.

"Tell me, love, what made you change your mind? You were so furious with me last night."

Bernadette smiled up at him. "Oh, something Lawrence asked me. He wanted to know if I'd have been happier if Doreen had turned out to be a real person. The question made me realize I was glad you'd made the whole thing up and that you were really in love with me."

Nick chuckled and rubbed his cheek contentedly against hers. "I knew Lawrence was a smart boy," he murmured.

Bernadette laughed softly and slipped her hands up on his shoulders. "About as smart as our children are going to be."

She felt his lips move into a happy smile. "There's one point I want to make about our children, Berny."

Bernadette leaned back to look at him. "Yes?"

"They won't have to be millionaires by the time they're thirty-five."

"Definitely not," she assured him, thinking how wonderful it was going to be to give him children, to give him her love.

"And they'll get to play sports and dance and wear T-shirts and tennis shoes. They may even have a dog running around in the house. They'll get to eat junk food and listen to rock music and all the other things I never got to do."

"They'll be typical kids," she whispered lovingly. "Just promise me one thing."

"Anything," he said, his arms tightening around her.

"That their father will always be here to love them and their mother."

"I wouldn't have it any other way," he said, his voice raw with emotion.

Bernadette sighed and met his searching lips. It was a long time before another word was said, and then it was Bernadette who spoke, her voice husky with desire.

"I didn't know an ultra-conservative businessman like you could be so sly and cunning, so sexy and endearing."

He smiled into her eyes. "You didn't? Maybe I should teach you."

She shook her head. Her hands slipped up his chest and undid a button on his shirt. "I've had enough teaching, Nick. Why don't you show me."

* * * * *

Silhouette **Romance**®

COMING NEXT MONTH

#658 A WOMAN IN LOVE—Brittany Young
When archaeologist Melina Chase met the mysterious Aristo Drapano aboard a treasure-hunting ship in the Greek isles, she knew he was her most priceless find....

#659 WALTZ WITH THE FLOWERS—Marcine Smith
When Estella Blaine applied for a loan to build a stable on her farm, she never expected bank manager Cody Marlowe to ask for her heart as collateral!

#660 IT HAPPENED ONE MORNING—Jill Castle
A chance encounter in the park with free-spirited dog trainer Collier Woolery had Neysa Williston's orderly heart spinning. Could he convince her that their meeting was destiny?

#661 DREAM OF A LIFETIME—Arlene James
Businessman Dan Wilson needed an adventure and found one in the Montana Rockies with lovely mountain guide Laney Scott. But now he wanted her to follow his trail....

#662 THE WEDDING MARCH—Terry Essig
Feisty five-foot Lucia Callahan had had just about enough of tall, protective men, and she set out to find a husband her own size...but she couldn't resist Daniel Statler—all six feet of him!

#663 NO WAY TO TREAT A LADY—Rita Rainville
Aunt Tillie was at it again, matchmaking between her llama-ranching nephew, Dave McGraw, and reading teacher Jennifer Hale. True love would never be the same again!

AVAILABLE THIS MONTH:

Coming in July from

Silhouette Desire®

ODD MAN OUT #505
by Lass Small

Roberta Lambert is too busy with her job to notice that her new apartment-mate is a strong, desirable man. But Graham Rawlins has ways of getting her undivided attention....

Roberta is one of five fascinating Lambert sisters. She is as enticing as each one of her three sisters, whose stories you have already enjoyed or will want to read:

- Hillary in GOLDILOCKS AND THE BEHR (Desire #437)

- Tate in HIDE AND SEEK (Desire #453)

- Georgina in RED ROVER (Desire #491)

Watch for Book IV of Lass Small's terrific miniseries and read Fredricka's story in TAGGED (Desire #528) coming in October.

You'll flip . . . your pages won't!
Read paperbacks *hands-free* with

Book Mate • I

The perfect "mate" for all your romance paperbacks

Traveling • Vacationing • At Work • In Bed • Studying • Cooking • Eating

Perfect size for all standard paperbacks, this wonderful invention makes reading a pure pleasure! Ingenious design holds paperback books OPEN and FLAT so even wind can't ruffle pages— leaves your hands free to do other things. Reinforced, wipe-clean vinyl-covered holder flexes to let you turn pages without undoing the strap . . . supports paperbacks so well, they have the strength of hardcovers!

Pages turn WITHOUT opening the strap.

SEE-THROUGH STRAP

Reinforced back stays flat.

Built in bookmark.

BOOK MARK

BACK COVER HOLDING STRIP

10" x 7¼", opened.
Snaps closed for easy carrying, too.